GRIMMS' FAIRY TALES

Translated and adapted by
PATRICIA CRAMPTON

Illustrated by
BENVENUTI

DERRYDALE BOOKS

NEW YORK

Contents

First published in 1970
By Editions des Deux Coqs d'Or, Paris
. under the title: *Contes de Grimm*

©1970 by Editions des Deux Coqs d'Or, Paris

This 1988 edition published
by Derrydale Books, distributed by Crown Publishers, Inc.,
225 Park Avenue South, New York, New York 10003,
by arrangement with Octopus Books Limited.

Printed by Mladinska knjiga, Yugoslavia

ISBN 0–517–67136–0

hgfedcba

THE FROG PRINCE

In the far-off days, when fairies brought people good luck (or bad!) there was a king who had a number of very beautiful daughters. But the youngest princess was even lovelier than her sisters – so lovely that the sun blinked when he looked at her.

There was a wood close to the palace, where the little princess loved to play in the shade of the trees when the day was hot.

Sitting beside a pool fed by a clear spring, she would toss up and catch her favourite toy, a golden ball, for hours on end.

One day she threw the ball too hard and instead of dropping back into her hand, it fell into the depths of the spring. Tears sprang to her eyes as she saw it vanish among the water weeds and soon she was sobbing her heart out.

'Why are you crying, princess?' said a tiny voice. 'All those tears would melt a stone!'

The princess looked everywhere, but all she could see was a frog, poking its head out of the water.

'So it was you!' she exclaimed. 'I'm crying because my golden ball has fallen into the spring.'

'Dry your tears!' said the frog. 'I can help you – but what will you give me for your golden ball?'

'Anything you like,' said the princess. 'My embroidered dresses, my pearls, my bracelets . . . even my golden crown!'

'I have no use for your embroidered dresses, your pearls, your bracelets, or even your golden crown. Marry me! I want to be your friend and play games with you; I want to share your meals, eat from your plate and drink from your glass. And at night I want to sleep in your bed. If you will promise me all that, I will dive for your golden ball.'

Why not, thought the princess. A frog can't live far from his pond and his friends. 'Yes, yes,' she cried. 'I will promise you all that, if only you will bring me my golden ball!'

The frog at once dived to the depths of the pool, picked the ball up in his mouth and swam back to the bank. He leaped over to the princess and dropped the ball at her feet.

The delighted princess picked it up and ran off through the wood without a thought for the little frog hopping painfully behind her, begging her to wait.

The next evening, when everyone at the palace was sitting in the dining-hall and the princess was tasting the delicacies placed on her silver dish, they heard a strange sound as something mounted the marble steps: *splish, splash!* Moments later, the same something was knocking at the door of the hall, croaking: 'Princess, pretty princess, open the door!'

The princess ran to the door and flung it open. To her alarm, a frog sat panting on the threshold. Slamming the door, she ran back to her seat trembling from head to foot.

'What is it, my child? Is there a giant at the door? Has he come for you?'

'No, no,' cried the princess, 'it's not a giant, it's a horrid frog!'

'And what does he want?'

'Oh, papa,' said the princess, bursting into tears, 'yesterday my golden ball fell into the spring. A frog heard me crying and promised to bring it back if I would marry him. I promised, but only because I thought it could never happen. And now he's here and he wants to come in.'

'Princess,' croaked the little voice at that moment, 'pretty princess let me in! Have you forgotten your promise?'

'A promise is a promise,' said the king sternly. 'Let him in!'

The princess had to do as she was told, and in hopped the frog, right up to the princess's chair.

'Pick me up,' he told her, 'and place me beside your plate.'

The princess hesitated, but the king ordered her to obey and the frog asked her to push her plate closer so that he could share her meal. While he ate with obvious pleasure, the princess had difficulty in swallowing a mouthful.

'I've had enough,' said the frog at last. ' I would like to go to bed now. Take me to your bedchamber and I will sleep on your pillow.'

The princess sobbed with anger and disgust. She could not bear to touch the ugly creature and the idea of sharing her bed with him made her feel quite sick.

8

'Obstinate child!' thundered the king. 'You were glad of the frog when you needed him, and you must not despise him now!'

The princess had to overcome her disgust and pick up the frog. Holding the creature between her thumb and first finger, she carried him to her room, dropped him in a corner and went to bed.

Up hopped the frog. 'I am tired too, princess. Make room for me, or I will speak to your father.'

'Ugh!' said the princess, but she had to obey.

The next morning, the little croaking voice spoke in her ear: 'Today, princess, we shall be married. Remember your promise!'

'I remember,' the little princess groaned, turning her back on the frog.

It was quite a different voice that made her open her eyes wide and look slowly round again.

'My princess,' said the new voice,' you have broken the spell and I am free.'

Gazing at her with loving eyes was a handsome prince, who held between his thumb and forefinger, just as the princess had done the night before, the spotted skin of a humble frog. A wicked fairy had cast a spell on him, which could not be broken until the frog had slept in a princess's bed and she had promised to marry him.

The prince and princess said goodbye to the king and all other princesses and set off for the prince's kingdom in a coach pulled by eight white horses with golden buckles on their harness and white ostrich feathers nodding on their heads. Henry, the prince's faithful servant, rode behind, his heart glowing with happiness.

When his young master had been turned into a frog the faithful servant's heart had burst and had to be held together by iron bands. Now the warmth of his joy melted the cracks together again and the iron bands fell off with such a clatter that for a moment the young couple thought the coach must be breaking up.

The story was told to me by my grandmother, and that is all she knew, but I am quite sure that the prince and princess lived happily ever after and had a family of six handsome princes and princesses who played together with a golden ball and were always very kind to frogs.

THE MUSICIANS OF BREMEN

There was once a donkey which had been a patient and faithful servant for many years, but when he grew too old to carry heavy loads his master decided not to feed him anymore. Instead of waiting to die of starvation, the donkey set off for Bremen to become a musician.

After only a few minutes' walk he espied at the bottom of the roadside ditch a miserable hound, puffing and panting as if he had been running too far and too fast.

'Why are you so short of breath, terror of the warrens?' asked the donkey.

'Ah me,' groaned the hound, 'I am old and tired, I cannot hunt and my master wants to shoot me. I have escaped, but what now? How am I to live?'

'Come along with me,' said the donkey. 'I'm going to be a lute-player in Bremen – you can bang the cymbals.'

When he had got his breath back the hound set off with the donkey.

They had not been walking long when they met a cat with a face as long as three rainy days.

'What's wrong, mouser of the mills?' asked the donkey.

'Who would have the heart to laugh, when his life's in danger?' moaned the cat. 'Just because I'm getting old and would rather purr by the fire than catch mice, my mistress tried to drown me. I escaped, but what can I do now?'

'Come with us,' said the donkey. 'We're going to Bremen to be strolling musicians. I'm sure you know all about night-time concerts.'

So the three of them walked on together. Soon they passed a gate where the farmyard cock perched, crowing his head off.

'What are you straining your throat for?' asked the donkey. 'You're hurting our ears!'

13

'It's Sunday tomorrow,' said the cock, 'and I'm to be put in the pot for my mistress's guests, so I'm singing while I can.'

'Come with us, Redpoll,' said the donkey. 'We're going to Bremen to be musicians and with your magnificent voice we'll be the fine foursome.'

Down hopped the cock and off they all went.

As night was falling they reached a forest, where they decided to spend the night. Donkey and dog lay down under a great oak, cat and cock settled in

the branches. Just as he was falling asleep the cock thought he glimpsed a light flickering in the distance.

'I can see a house!' he told his friends.

'Off we go, then,' said the donkey. 'We're not too comfortable here.'

When they reached the house they found it oddly sinister, in spite of the lighted window. The donkey, being the tallest, looked in.

'What can you see, Greybeard?' asked the cock.

'I can see some robbers enjoying a splendid feast,' said the donkey.

'I wouldn't mind that,' said the cock.

'Nor I,' said the donkey, 'but we haven't been invited.'

So they squatted down under the window and thought out a plan.

The donkey wedged his front hoofs on the window ledge, the dog jumped up on his back, the cat scrambled on to the dog's back and the cock perched on the cat's head. Then all four of them began to sing out, each in his own

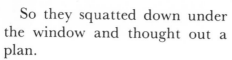

fashion; the donkey brayed, the dog barked, the cat miaowed and the cock crowed. Then they all burst into the room in a shower of broken glass.

The robbers leaped to their feet in terror and rushed into the forest as if the devil were at their heels.

What a feast for the four friends! They ate as if they had not eaten for a month and when they were fully satisfied they blew out the candles and settled down again, the donkey in the courtyard, the dog by the back door, the cat by the hearth and the cock on the roof beam. Tired and well-fed as they were, they were very soon asleep.

Towards midnight the robbers plucked up their courage and stole (they were good at that) back to the house, which was now dark and silent.

'We shouldn't have been so easily scared!' said their chief. He sent one of their number ahead to spy out the land.

The robber made his way to the fireplace to light a lamp. The cat's eyes glowed in the darkness – burning embers so the thief thought, but when he tried to light a taper from them, the cat sprang at his face, clawing and spitting. The terrified robber stumbled to the back door, but the dog jumped up and bit him in the calf, and as he crossed the courtyard at full speed the donkey gave him a fearful kick. Startled awake by the row, the cock began to crow: 'Cock-a-doodle-doo! Cock-a-doodle-doo!'

When he reached the rest of the gang the robber's teeth were chattering so violently that he could barely speak.

'There's a ho-ho-horrible witch by the fire,' he stuttered. 'She spat at me and scratched my face with her crooked finger-nails. The m-m-man at the door slashed my leg with his knife. In the courtyard a black mo-mo-monster sent me flying with a tremendous blow. And from the upper window their chief was shouting: "Stop the noodle, do! Stop the noodle, do!" I was lucky to get away with my life.'

The robbers never went near the house again, but as for the four musicians, they liked it so much that they decided to stay, and for all I know they are living there still.

THE SEVEN RAVENS

There was once a man who had seven children, all boys. He longed for a daughter, so when their eighth child was born they were overjoyed that it was a girl.

But for all their joy, they were worried because the child was so small and frail. They decided to have her baptised immediately and the father told one of his sons to run to the spring for water. All his brothers decided to race him there, but when they all arrived at the same time there was a violent scuffle and the jug fell on to the rocks where it smashed into a thousand pieces.

What would their father say! Too frightened to face his fury, the boys stayed where they were.

'The little fools!' cried their father, beside himself with impatience. 'They've forgotten the way home and they're playing games!'

After an hour his anxiety for his baby daughter made him lose his temper completely. 'They're nothing but birdbrains,' he shouted. 'I just wish they were a lot of ravens!'

No sooner had he spoken than there was a rush of wings as seven jet-black ravens flapped over his head, rose into the sky and disappeared.

The seven sons had gone and their parents grieved over them, but they were comforted a little by the blossoming health and beauty of their little daughter.

As the years passed the girl was unaware that she had any brothers, because her parents took care never to speak of them. But one day she overheard some

neighbours talking: 'That's a sweet girl, right enough,' they said. 'All the same, it's thanks to her that her parents lost seven fine sons!'

The astonished child ran to her parents. 'Did I have seven brothers? What became of them?' she cried, and her parents could no longer keep their secret from her.

From that day on the girl could think of nothing but her brothers and the spell that had been cast on them. 'It's my fault, I know it's all my fault,' she would whisper into her pillow every night, until one morning she made up her mind to go and find her brothers, wherever they might be. Taking nothing but a loaf, a gourd full of fresh water and her mother's ring for remembrance, she set out and walked to the ends of the earth.

No one lived there but the Sun, the Moon and the Stars and it was to the Sun that the young girl went first. The heat was terrible.

'What do you want?' blazed the Sun. 'I cook little girls and eat them!'

Running for dear life, the girl took refuge with the Moon, but the pale, cold creature was just as nasty as the Sun. 'I smell hot blood to warm my bones!' groaned the Moon, and the young girl took to her heels again, seeking this time the protection of the Stars.

The Stars were kind and sympathetic. They sat round the girl in a circle, listened to her story and decided to help her to find her brothers. The Morning Star rose and handed her a little bone.

'Take this,' he said, 'it is the key that will open the door to the glass mountain where your brothers are now.'

The girl wrapped the bone in her handkerchief and set off for the distant glass mountain. The way was long and hard, but her heart was full of courage and she reached it at last. But, oh horror! when she unwrapped her handkerchief, the bone, the good Star's gift, had gone and she could not unlock the door. The brave little girl did not hesitate; she took out her knife, cut off her finger and put it in the lock. The door opened and she went into the mountain.

A little dwarf came to meet her. 'What do you want, my girl?' he asked.

'I'm looking for my brothers, the seven ravens,' she told him.

'My lords the Ravens are not here just now,' said the dwarf, 'but if you would like to wait for them, please come in.'

The young girl stepped into a room where a table was set with seven small plates and seven small goblets. The girl took a morsel of food from each plate and a sip of wine from each goblet, but into the seventh goblet she slipped her mother's ring.

Suddenly she heard the rushing of wings.

'My lords the Ravens have returned,' said the dwarf.

The girl hid behind the door as the hungry ravens entered and hopped on to the table. 'Who's been eating from my plate? Who's been drinking from my goblet? A human being has been here!' they cried, one after another.

Then the seventh raven spied his mother's ring at the bottom of his goblet.

'The Lord be praised!' he cried. 'If our little sister is here we shall be released from the spell!'

As she stepped from her hiding place, the ravens regained their human form.

How they kissed and hugged and wept for joy – and how their parents rejoiced to see them all come home again!

HANSEL AND GRETEL

O nce upon a time there was a poor woodcutter who lived on the edge of a great forest. He had a son called Hansel and a daughter called Gretel. Their mother had died when the children were small and the woodcutter had married an evil woman who had no love for the two children.

The woodcutter could scarcely earn enough to keep his family and in a poor year there was often no food at all in their wretched cabin. One night when he was tossing and turning, unable to sleep for worry, he groaned aloud:

'What is to become of us? How are we to feed our children, when we have not enough to eat ourselves?'

'Listen, husband,' said his wife, 'we have only to take them deep into the forest tomorrow morning. We will light a fire for them and give them each a little of our remaining bread and then we will leave them while we cut wood. They will never find their way home and we shall be rid of them for ever.'

'No, wife,' said the woodcutter, 'I shall never do that. How could I have the heart to abandon my children in a forest full of wild beasts?'

'Idiot!' said his wife. 'Very well, all four of us may as well starve! Why don't you plane some wood for our coffins?'

She nagged and nagged, until the heavy-hearted father agreed to her plan.

In the room next door, Hansel and Gretel were also unable to sleep for hunger and they heard the whole conversation.

'This is the end of us,' said Gretel.

'Quiet!' said Hansel, 'Stop crying and trust me. I will find a way.'

When he was certain that their parents were asleep, Hansel slipped out of bed, pulled on his jacket and stole outside. The night was clear and cold and the full moon turned the white pebbles outside the door to silver. Hansel filled his pockets with pebbles and returned to bed.

At dawn their stepmother came to wake the children.

'Up, lazybones!' she said. 'We are going to fetch wood from the forest.'

She gave each a morsel of bread, advising them not to eat it before noon, since it was all they would have for the day. Hansel's pockets were full of pebbles, so Gretel put the two pieces of bread in her apron.

As they walked, the little boy stopped from time to time and looked around.

22

'What are you looking at, Hansel?' asked his father. 'Stop lagging behind!'

'Oh, Papa,' said Hansel, 'I'm looking at my little white cat on the roof of the house, waving me goodbye.'

'Little fool,' said his stepmother, 'that is not your cat, it is nothing but a sunbeam shining on the chimney.'

But in fact Hansel was looking back at the white pebbles that he was scattering along the way.

When they were far enough into the forest their father stopped.

'Collect some dead wood,' he told them. 'I'm going to light a fire for you so that you will not be cold, and you must wait for us here while we cut some branches further off.'

Hansel and Gretel collected kindling and dry wood, which soon blazed up merrily, and sat down beside the fire. When the sun was directly over their heads they ate their pieces of bread. They thought they could hear axe-blows not far away, but it was not the woodcutter's axe, it was a broken branch, which was striking the trunk of a tree at every puff of wind.

Tired after the long walk, Hansel and Gretel soon fell into a deep sleep and when they woke up again the fire had been out for some time and darkness had already fallen. Gretel began to cry.

'How shall we get out of the forest?' she sobbed.

'Don't worry,' said Hansel, 'as soon as the moon is up we shall be able to see the way clearly enough.'

It was not long before the moon shone down through the trees, making the pebbles that Hansel had scattered on the way shine bright as silver coins. The little boy took his sister by the hand and they followed the pebbles home, reaching the house at daybreak. Their stepmother opened the door.

'Naughty children!' she screeched. 'Why did you sleep so long in the forest? We thought you did not want to come home!' She was secretly angry that they had returned.

But the poor woodcutter was delighted to see his children again and regretted leaving them behind.

Not long afterwards there was famine in the land once more and one evening the children heard their stepmother nagging the woodcutter yet again:

'We have scarcely a mouthful of bread left. What are we to do when that has gone? We must get rid of the children; we must lead them even further into the forest.'

'It would be better to give them my share,' said their poor father; but as he had given in the first time, his wife just kept on nagging until he gave way a second time. The woodcutter was not a wicked man, but he was weak and allowed his wife to order him about.

When their parents were asleep Hansel got up as he had done before, but when he tried to go out he found that his stepmother had locked the door and he was unable to gather pebbles.

'Don't despair,' he told Gretel. 'The Lord will help us, never fear!'

The next morning their stepmother came to rouse the children very early, giving each an even smaller morsel of bread than before.

As they walked Hansel crumbled the bread in his pocket and dropped the crumbs along the way.

'What are you looking at, Hansel?' asked his father. 'Why are you lagging behind?'

'Oh, Papa,' said the little boy, 'I'm looking at my pigeon perched on the roof, calling goodbye to me.'

'Little fool,' said his stepmother, 'that is not your pigeon, it is simply the rising sun shining on the chimney!'

In fact Hansel was only looking back at the crumbs he had scattered on the path.

They walked for a long time, far longer than before, until they were in a part of the forest which the children did not know at all. When they stopped, their father once again lit a big fire and his wife told the children:

'Sit down by the fire and rest. You can go to sleep if you like, while we cut wood. We will fetch you this evening when we have finished work.'

Towards midday Gretel shared her little bit of bread with her brother, as he had left all his on the path. Then they fell asleep and no one came to waken them. When they opened their eyes it was pitch-black night.

'Wait until the moon is up,' said Hansel, trying to comfort his sister. 'Then we shall see the breadcrumbs I have scattered and find our way home.'

When the moon rose they set off, but they did not find a single one of Hansel's crumbs. The birds of the forest had eaten them all up.

'Never fear,' said Hansel, 'we shall find our way home in the end!'

But even when they had walked all night and the whole of the next day they could not find a way out of the forest. They had nothing to eat but a few wild berries that were left on the bushes and they became so weak that in the end they could scarcely walk.

They fell asleep at the foot of a tree and did their best to set out again next morning, but they were at the end of their strength.

Towards midday they saw a little bird, as white as snow, perched on a branch and singing so prettily that the children stopped to listen. When it had finished singing the bird flapped its wings and flew away. It alighted on a bush a little way off and looked back at the children.

'Look, Hansel,' cried his sister, 'I think he's asking us to follow him!' They started to walk behind the bird and soon arrived at a clearing where there was a strange little house, on whose roof the bird perched. Hansel and Gretel had never seen a house like it: the walls were made of gingerbread, the roof of biscuit and the windows of candysugar.

'Oh, how good it looks!' cried Hansel. 'At last we shall be able to eat. I shall start with the roof. Try a bit of this window, Gretel, it's made of sugar!'

Hansel broke off a corner of the roof which was not far from the ground and crunched the biscuit, while Gretel took a little piece of window-pane. Then a shrill voice chanted from inside the house:

'Crack, crack, crunch!
My house who dares to munch?'

'It's the wind, it's the wind,' said the children, and went on eating.

Hansel found the roof delicious and broke off a larger piece, while Gretel took out the whole of one round window and settled comfortably on the ground to eat it.

At that moment the door opened and a horrible old woman appeared. She was bent double and supported herself on a crutch. Terrified by her appearance the children dropped what they were eating, but the old woman spoke to them in a sugary voice:

'Good-day, little ones,' she said. 'Since you have come this far, come right in; I will do you no harm!'

Taking them both by the hand she led them inside, where a delicious meal was already laid: milk, jam and sugar pancakes, apples and nuts. Hansel and Gretel gladly ate everything she gave them. Then, since they were dropping with sleep, she took them to a room where two dear little white beds were

already made up. Hansel and Gretel lay down, thinking themselves in paradise.

Now, the old woman was really a wicked witch who well knew how to disguise her wickedness with sweet words. Her house was built of gingerbread and biscuits simply to attract children, and soon as she caught one she would cook it and eat it.

Witches have very poor eyesight because of their red eyes, but their sense of smell is as good as a dog's and she could smell people coming. As Hansel and Gretel approached the cottage the witch had sniggered:

'Those two are mine:
How well I shall dine!'

Next morning she went to look at the sleeping children. How deliciously tasty they looked, with their fresh, pink cheeks!

'What choice morsels,' she murmured, licking her lips. She picked up Hansel without waking him and shut him in a hen-coop where, cry as he would, no one would come to help him.

'Get up, good-for-nothing,' she shouted. 'Fetch water and make a good meal for your brother in the hen-coop. I'm going to fatten him up and when he's fat enough, I shall eat him!'

Gretel shed bitter tears, but she had to obey the wicked witch because she would not desert her brother.

Every morning the old woman hobbled to the hen-coop.

'Show me your finger,' she told Hansel. 'I want to see if you're getting fat.'

Through the bars Hansel would hold out a little chicken bone, to deceive the witch with her bad eyesight, but when after a whole month he did not seem to have fattened up at all, the witch lost patience.

'Gretel,' she shouted, 'fetch water and fill the cauldron. Thin or fat I'm going to eat your brother now!'

Gretel obeyed, sobbing.

'Oh, if only the wild beasts had eaten us – at least we would have died together! Help us, dear Lord!'

'Stop your whining,' said the witch. 'It will do you no good. Light the fire and hurry. I'm hungry! I've made the dough and I'm going to make my bread first. Get into the oven and see if it's hot enough.'

The wicked witch thought she had only to shut the oven door and then she could cook Gretel and eat her too, but the little girl knew better.

'I've never been in there,' she objected. 'I don't know what to do.'

'Little goose,' said the old woman, 'it's quite easy. Look – even I can get in.'

So saying, she plunged her head and shoulders into the oven and, as quick as light, Gretel seized her by the leg and tipped her in. Then she slammed the iron door and shot the bolt. Heedless of the witch's shrieks, Gretel left her to cook to a cinder while she ran to release her brother.

'We're saved, Hansel!' she cried. 'The witch is dead.'

Wild with joy, the two children kissed and danced about. Then they explored the gingerbread house from top to bottom, opening all its treasure chests which were filled with pearls and precious stones.

'These are better than pebbles,' said Hansel, filling his pockets, while Gretel filled her apron.

'Let us go now,' said Hansel, 'and never enter this forest again. It is bewitched!'

30

After two hours' walk they reached a wide river, but could see no bridge or boat on which to cross. Only a white swan was floating on the quiet water.

'Perhaps he would help us,' said Gretel. 'I will call him:

> Oh swan, lovely swan, with your neck so white,
> Help Hansel and Gretel out of their plight!'

The swan floated to the bank and Hansel climbed on his back.

'Climb on behind me, little sister,' said Hansel, but Gretel refused.

'Together we would be too heavy. I shall wait here and the swan will carry us across one by one.'

When they were both on the other side of the river they thanked the swan, which bowed with such a noble air that they were convinced he must be an enchanted prince.

It was not long before they reached places they seemed to recognise, until at last they saw the woodcutter's house through the trees. They ran to it and threw themselves on their father, who kissed them, weeping for joy. The poor man had been tormented with remorse since the day when he had left Hansel and Gretel in the forest, and even the death of his wicked wife had brought him no peace.

When Hansel emptied his pockets and Gretel her apron so that the pearls and precious stones rolled across the ground, the three of them knew they were safe from want for ever and settled down to live happily ever after.

THE GOLDEN GOOSE

There was once a man who had three sons. The youngest was the constant butt of his brothers, who thought him of no account and treated him like a fool. In fact, that was what they called him.

One morning, when the eldest set off to cut wood in the forest, his mother gave him a crusty, buttered roll and a bottle of good wine to quench his thirst. As he entered the forest he met a little old man.

'Won't you give me a bit of your roll and a little wine to drink?' said the little man. 'I'm weak with hunger and thirst.'

But the young man was not generous.

'If I let you have part of my roll and wine I shall not have enough left for myself,' he said. 'On your way!'

His selfishness was soon paid for – the little old man saw to that. As he was chopping a tree truck his axe slipped, he cut his arm and had to hurry home to have it dressed.

The next morning it was the second son's turn to take the forest road. Like his brother, he was given a crusty, golden buttered roll and a bottle of good wine to take with him. He too met the little old man, who asked him for a bite of roll and some wine to drink. But like his brother, he had no heart.

'Some for you, less for me,' he said. 'On your way!'

His punishment was not long in coming. After only a few blows his axe slipped and cut his leg. He had considerable difficulty in getting home to his parents.

'Let me take my turn at woodcutting,' said Dummling next morning.

'Your brothers had no luck,' said his father, 'so how do you expect to succeed? No, no, you're too foolish.'

But Dummling pestered him until at last his father gave in.

His mother gave him a half-baked roll and a bottle of bad beer. On the edge of the wood Dummling met the little old man.

'Won't you give me a bit of your roll and let me drink from your bottle?' said the little man. 'I'm weak with hunger and thirst.'

'I have only a half-baked roll and some sour beer,' said Dummling, 'but if that will do, take it with all my heart. Let's sit down and share it.'

So they sat down and shared, and Dummling discovered that his badly baked bread had become a crusty, golden buttered roll and that his bad beer had turned into good wine. When they had eaten and drunk with pleasure, the little man spoke:

'You have such a kind heart and are so ready to share what you have that I would like to make you happy. You see this old oak tree? Chop it down and you will find something under its roots.'

Dummling did as he said, and under the roots of the tree he found a goose with golden feathers. He tucked it under his arm and walked out into the wide world. That night he came to an inn, where he decided to spend the night.

The innkeeper had three daughters who were amazed to see such an unusual bird.

'I'd like the chance to pluck one of its golden feathers!' said the eldest, and waiting until Dummling had gone to bed, she picked up the goose and tried to pluck out one of its feathers. But her hands stuck to the bird and, try as she might, she could not let go.

The second sister had followed her, also planning to pluck a golden feather. She reached the goose, but her hand brushed her sister's in passing and at once the two were fixed together.

When the youngest daughter entered the room her sisters burst out:

'Keep away from us, for the love of heaven, keep away!'

But the youngest thought:

'They're getting goose feathers for themselves – why shouldn't I?'

She seized her sister by the skirt, but in the same instant her hand was stuck; the three sisters had to spend the night with the goose, quite unable to let go of each other.

Next morning Dummling tucked his goose under his arm and marched off without paying any attention to the three captives at his heels. The unfortunate girls had to follow wherever he went; now this way, now that, as the fancy took him. After walking for an hour or two they met the village pastor.

'Where are you going, you silly girls?' he exclaimed. 'Aren't you ashamed, running after a boy like this?'

He put his hand on the shoulder of the youngest, but no sooner had he touched her than his hand stuck fast. Now he too had to follow the boy. After a time they met the sexton, who was astonished to see the pastor taking part in such tomfoolery.

'Hey, hey, your reverence,' he shouted, 'where are you going so fast? Don't forget that there's a christening today!'

He tugged at the pastor's coat, but the moment he touched it he was stuck fast and had to follow them as well.

Two peasants returning from the fields, their mattocks over their shoulders, watched the little procession in surprise. The pastor called on them to release him and his sexton, but as soon as they touched the sexton they were stuck and had to follow the rest. There were now seven people following the boy with the golden goose.

Trotting fast, they reached the capital of the kingdom. The king had a daughter who was so serious that no one could even make her smile. Her worried father had issued a proclamation that very day, promising his daughter in marriage to the first man who could make her laugh.

Dummling set off at once for the palace, with his goose under his arm and the whole motley crew stuck to the goose.

As soon as she saw the ridiculous string of captives trotting head to tail behind Dummling and his goose, the princess began to laugh so hard that it seemed she would never stop. So Dummling asked the king for her hand in marriage, but the king did not think much of him as a son-in-law.

'To win the princess you must find me a man who can drink a barrel of wine all by himself!'

Dummling remembered the little man who had given him the goose and went back to the forest to find him. By the old oak tree he found a man who was looking very sorry for himself.

'What is troubling you, friend?' said Dummling.

'I'm dying of thirst,' said the man. 'There seems to be a burning stone in my stomach and I would go up in steam if I drank cold water. I've already emptied a barrel of wine, but it scarcely wetted my throat.'

'I can do something for you,' said Dummling. 'Just come along with me.'

Dummling took the man to the king's cellars, where he emptied cask after cask, until there was not a drop left.

'Find me a man who can eat a mountain of bread on his own!' he told Dummling, and this time the young man ran straight back to the fallen oak.

There he found a gloomy-looking man who was tightening his belt, notch by notch.

'I've eaten all the bread at the baker's shop,' he told Dummling, 'but with a hunger like this, what use are a few loaves to me?'

'Get up and follow me,' said Dummling cheerfully. 'You shall eat to your heart's content.'

The king had ordered that all the flour in the kingdom should be made into dough and baked in a loaf as big as a mountain, but by nightfall the hungry man had finished the lot.

Yet once again, when Dummling claimed his bride, the king refused:

'Find me a boat which can sail on land and sea, and you shall have my daughter's hand,' he told Dummling.

Off went Dummling to the forest, and this time the little old man was waiting for him by the fallen oak.

'Thanks to you, I did not go hungry or thirsty,' he said. 'To repay your kindness I am going to give you the boat you need.'

Dummling travelled overland to the palace with all sails set and this time the king gave him his daughter's hand at last.

So Dummling and the princess were married, and when the king died they reigned happily together for many years.

RAPUNZEL

Once upon a time there lived a husband and wife who had always wanted a child, and one day their wish was granted.

Now, next door to their house there was garden full of beautiful flowers and tasty vegetables, but the garden was surrounded by high walls and no one ever tried to enter it, because it belonged to a wicked witch.

From an upstairs window the wife could see the garden quite well, and while she waited for her baby to arrive she began to long for a special kind of vegetable that grew there, which was called rapunzel. As the days went by, she began to dislike all other foods, and grew so thin and pale that her husband was deeply troubled.

'Is there nothing you really want?' he asked her.

'Oh, husband,' she sobbed, 'all I want is some of the rapunzel from the witch's garden. If I can't have it, I shall die of hunger.'

That very night her husband climbed over the wall and picked a big handful of rapunzel, which he took back to his grateful wife. Unfortunately she liked the stuff so much that the next day she wanted even more than before. Her husband climbed over the wall again and hastily pulled up several handfuls of rapunzel, but when he stood up to go, he came face to face with the witch.

'How dare you come into my garden!' she shrieked. 'Been stealing, too, I see. This will cost you dear, I promise you!'

'Spare me!' cried the man, trembling all over. 'I had to do it for my poor wife, who is expecting our first child.'

'Oh, in that case, take what you want,' said the witch, but she was only pretending to be kind, for she went on: 'All I ask is that you give me the child as soon as it is born.'

The poor husband was so frightened of losing his wife that he agreed, and when their little girl was a week old the witch arrived to collect the child, whom she named Rapunzel. The girl grew more beautiful with every day that passed and when she was twelve years old the witch shut her up in a tower in the heart of the forest. When she came to feed the girl, she would stand under the one little window in the tower and call:

'Rapunzel, Rapunzel, let down your hair!'

Rapunzel had the most wonderful hair, very long and like a golden rope. When the witch called her she uncoiled her crown of plaits, knotted them to the window post and let them down for the witch to climb up.

One day, when the king's son was hunting in the forest, he happened to ride by Rapunzel's tower. He paused at the sound of a sweet voice singing – it was Rapunzel, trying to fill her lonely hours. The prince longed to enter the tower and speak to the owner of that sweet voice, but he could find no way in. He returned to the palace, but he could not forget the girl's voice and day after day he returned to the foot of the tower to hear her singing.

One morning while he was listening, sitting in a nearby tree, he saw the old witch come to the foot of the tower and shout:

'Rapunzel, Rapunzel, let down your hair!'

The prince was dumbfounded at the sight of the long golden plaits uncoiling from the little window for the witch to climb up. The next day, when he returned to the forest the prince went to the foot of the tower and called:

'Rapunzel, Rapunzel, let down your hair!'

The plaits were let down and the king's son climbed up to the window. At

first Rapunzel was terrified to see a stranger coming in, but after he had told his story she was so touched by his faithfulness that all her fears vanished.

'I fell in love with your voice,' the prince told her, 'and now that I have seen you, I love you with all my heart. Will you be my wife?'

Rapunzel found the prince both handsome and gentle. 'I cannot fail to be happier with him than with the witch!' she thought, and she promised to marry the prince.

'I would like to go away with you now,' she said, 'but I have no way of leaving the tower. If you will bring me a skein of silk every day, I will plait a rope long enough to help me escape.'

So every day the prince went to visit Rapunzel, and their love for each other grew apace. The witch noticed nothing, until the day when Rapunzel exclaimed thoughtlessly:

'How can you take so long to climb up, when the king's son is here in the twinkling of an eye?'

'You little cheat!' cried the witch. 'You have deceived me, have you? This will cost you dear!'

Taking out her scissors, she seized Rapunzel's plaits and chopped them off. Then, for like all powerful witches she could fly, she carried Rapunzel off to a distant desert and left her alone.

The same evening the witch returned to the tower and bound the girl's tresses firmly to the window post. When the prince called Rapunzel, the witch lowered the ropes of hair and the prince climbed up as usual, only to be met at the top by the hateful mockery of the old witch.

'The cage is empty,' she cackled. 'The bird has flown and you will never hear her song again. The cat's got her – and it's going to scratch your eyes out, too!'

The distraught prince let go of the tresses and plunged down on to a thorn bush which broke his fall and saved his life. Alas, those same thorns scratched his eyes as well. The prince was blind! From that day on he wandered through the forest, feeding on roots and wild berries and drinking from streams.

Years passed and all the time, though he did not know it, the prince was walking towards Rapunzel's desert refuge.

One day, as he wandered sadly through the desert, the prince heard a sweet voice that he seemed to know. Rapunzel saw him coming, recognised him and embraced him tenderly, shedding tears of joy. Two of her tears fell on the prince's eyes, which at once regained their sight.

In great happiness they made their way to the palace, where the old king rejoiced at the return of the son he had thought lost for ever.

After all their adventures, Rapunzel and her prince lived happily for many more years.

JORINDA AND JORINGEL

Once upon a time there was an old woman who lived all alone in a grand castle in the heart of a dense forest. The old woman was a witch: by daylight she turned herself into a cat or an owl, but at night she took on human form again. She had the power to attract wild beasts and birds which she killed and then boiled or roasted for dinner.

The witch cast her spell on people as well as animals. If they approached within a hundred paces of the castle they stopped as if turned to stone, unable to move a muscle until the witch released them. Most people were released quite quickly, but if ever a pure young girl came near, the witch did not hesitate: she turned the girl into a bird and put her in a cage inside the castle. Up to now, she had captured nearly seven thousand birds.

One day a beautiful girl named Jorinda was walking in the forest with a handsome young man called Joringel.

'We must keep away from the castle!' said Joringel.

The turtle doves cooed, the shadows of the forest were brightened by the rays of the setting sun, yet the lovers were overwhelmed by sadness.

'Alas,' cried Jorinda, 'even in your presence, my heart is so heavy that I feel my death is near!'

The two had wandered so far that they had lost their way, and as Joringel tried to find the right path, he suddenly saw through the bushes the high walls of the witch's castle. At that very moment his veins turned to ice as he heard Jorinda singing a strange, sad song:

My little russet-throated bird,
My turtle-dove,
Sings of his woes, sings of his woes,
Sings to his love.
Sings to his love that he must die,
Sings of his . . . tirralee! tirralee!

Joringel turned. Jorinda had vanished, and from a branch a nightingale sang: 'Tirralee! Tirralee!'

A golden-eyed owl glided from the tree and circled Joringel three times, hooting 'Too-whit, Too-whoo!' From that moment Joringel was unable to make the slightest movement. It was as if he had been turned to stone.

As the sun disappeared, the owl turned into a bent old woman, with red eyes and a nose so hooked it touched her chin. Muttering and mumbling, she seized the nightingale and carried it away under Joringel's despairing eyes.

After a few minutes the witch returned. 'Hail, Beelzebub,' she hissed. 'When the moonlight falls on the nightingale's cage, let the boy go free!'

The spell that had bound Joringel was broken, but in anguish he threw himself at the old witch's feet.

'Give me back my Jorinda!' he implored her, but the witch said only: 'You will never see your beloved again!'

The heartbroken young man left the forest and walked until he reached a village he did not know, on the far side of the castle walls. There he took work as a shepherd taking care not to cross the enchanted barrier.

One night he had a strange dream. He had found a crimson flower at whose heart lay a great pearl. He picked it and entered the witch's castle and everything the flower touched was released from the witch's spell.

When he woke up the next morning, Joringel set out, in search of the magic flower. For nine days he tramped the hills and valleys in vain. On the tenth day he found the crimson flower, bearing at its heart a drop of dew as luminous as a pearl. Joringel picked the flower and hurried with it to the castle. He crossed the magic circle, but no harm came to him. He touched the great wrought-iron gates with the flower and they opened wide. In the middle of the courtyard he stopped to listen and the sound of the singing of birds guided him to the hall where the cages stood. There was the witch, busy feeding her seven thousand birds.

At the sight of Joringel the witch flew into a blind fury. Swearing, spitting, springing at him with cruel claws, she could not come within two paces of the magic flower. Ignoring her, Joringel began to search through the cages for the nightingale that had once been Jorinda. Suddenly he spied the witch, trying to steal away unnoticed with a little cage under her arm.

'Stop!' he cried, and in one leap he had reached her and touched her with the flower. The witch stood rooted to the spot, as she had made so many others do before, while Joringel touched the nightingale and Jorinda appeared, more beautiful than ever. Hand in hand, they walked round with the magic flower, releasing all the other young girls from the spell.

Their work of mercy done, they left the castle and returned home, where they married and lived happily for many years.

50

TABLE,
LAY
YOURSELF

Once upon a time there was a tailor who lived in a poor little cottage with his three sons. Their only valuable possession was a goat which ensured that they would not die of hunger, so they took great care of the creature.

One morning it was the eldest son's turn to take the goat out to graze. He led it to the church close, where the grass was green and juicy and the goat grazed and gambolled there all day long. That evening, the boy asked her: 'Have you had enough to eat?'

And the goat replied:

'I have eaten so much that I could not swallow another blade of grass, be-e-eh, be-e-eh!'

'Let's go home then,' said the young man.

As soon as they returned, his father said:

'Have you made sure the goat is well fed?'

'Oh, yes father,' said the boy. 'I only brought her home when she could not eat any more.'

The tailor was suspicious, so he went to the stable and asked the goat:

'Did you get enough to eat today, little nanny-goat?'

'Be-e-eh, be-e-eh!' said the goat, 'all I had were a few miserable tussocks of grass by the roadside! How could I possibly have had enough to eat?'

The furious tailor snatched up his long tailor's ruler and brought it down violently on his son's shoulders.

'Liar!' he cried, 'take that! So you'd deceive me would you? Be off then! Leave this house!'

Next morning it was the turn of the second son to take the goat out to graze. He led it to a grassy meadow full of flowers where the goat grazed and gambolled all day long. That evening, like his brother the night before, the young man asked:

'Have you had enough to eat?'

And as before, the goat replied:

'I have eaten so much that I could not swallow another blade of grass, be-e-eh, be-e-eh!'

'Let's go home, then,' said the young man.

As soon as he saw his father, the tailor asked:

'Have you made sure the goat is well fed?'

'Oh, yes father,' said the boy. 'I only brought her home when she should not eat any more.'

But once again, the tailor was not convinced, so he went to the stable, patted the goat and asked:

'Did you have enough to eat today, my little nanny-goat?'

'Be-e-eh, be-e-eh!' said the goat, 'all I had were a few miserable tussocks of grass by the roadside! How could I possibly have had enough to eat?'

The tailor was enraged to find that he had been cheated a second time. Seizing his ruler, he beat his second son harder than the first.

'You scoundrel!' he shouted, 'How could you have the heart to let such a sweet animal die of starvation? You're a liar too and I never want to see you again! Get out of here!'

On the third day the youngest son, not wanting to upset his father, decided to take the goat to some leafy bushes where she could graze to her heart's content. All day long the goat stuffed herself with the tasty, tender leaves. That evening, like his brother, the boy asked:

'Have you had enough to eat?'

And once again the goat answered:

'I have eaten so much that I could not swallow another leaf, be-e-eh, be-e-eh!'

'Let's go home then,' said the young man.

As soon as he saw his father, the tailor asked:

'Have you fed the goat well?'

'Oh yes, father,' said the boy, 'I only brought her home when she could not eat any more.'

But the tailor had no more confidence in his youngest son than in the others and he went to the stable to speak to the goat.

'Well, have you had enough to eat today, my little nanny-goat?' he asked, stroking the goat.

'Be-e-eh, be-e-eh,' said the the wicked animal, 'all I had were a few miserable tussocks of grass by the roadside! How could I possibly have had enough to eat?'

The tailor ran back to the house and beat the poor boy soundly.

'Be off, good-for-nothing!' he shouted. 'You have deceived me, like your brothers. You deserve no better fate than they!'

So the tailor was left alone with his goat and the next morning it was he who had to take the animal to graze.

'Come, my little nanny-goat,' he said, hugging and kissing the beast, 'today I am taking you out myself.'

And he took her to a fine, leafy thicket of the kind that goats love.

'Eat your fill,' he said, 'there's more here than you could ever need.'

All day long the goat grazed and gambolled in the thicket.

'Have you had enough to eat?' the tailor asked that evening.

'I have eaten so much,' said the goat, 'that I could not swallow another blade of grass, be-e-eh, be-e-eh!'

'Let's go home then,' said the tailor.

He took his goat to the stable and tied her up carefully.

'Have you had enough to eat?' he asked for the last time, just as he was leaving her.

But this time the goat replied, as she had on the previous evening;

'Be-e-eh, be-e-eh, all I had were a few miserable tussocks of grass by the roadside! How could I possibly have had enough to eat?'

At these words the tailor saw his mistake; he had called his sons liars and sent them packing when it was all the goat's fault!

'Just you wait, you monster!' he cried. 'You shall pay for this. You've got a bad time coming, you villainous goat!'

The tailor ran to fetch water, shaving soap and his razor. He soaped the goat and shaved it until there was not a single hair left on its head. Then he picked up a whip and beat it until it was black and blue, but the goat managed to break its rope and take flight from his blows.

Now the tailor was quite alone, dreaming sadly of his three sons out in the wide world. He would have been overjoyed to see them again, but no one knew what had become of them.

Now the eldest had found a position as a joiner's apprentice. He was a good worker and when the time came for him to leave, his master offered him a little

table in payment for his services. The table looked rough and ugly, but in reality it was a magic table. As soon as anyone said 'Little table, lay yourself!' it was immediately covered with a fine white cloth on which appeared a plate, a knife, a fork and a glass filled to the brim with rosy red wine, the very sight of which gladdened the heart. And that was not all: there were also dishes with roast beef, ham, chicken and fresh vegetables.

'With a table like this I shall never want again.' said the young man. 'I shall not even have to pay to eat at an inn.'

Every evening he would settle down in a field or at the edge of a wood, set up his table in front of him and say: 'Little table, lay yourself!' and instantly the table was covered with all the good things he could wish for.

'Perhaps I should go back to my father now,' he thought one day. 'His anger must have died down and he may be pleased to see me, especially with my magic table.'

The young man set off for his own village, but when he was only an hour or two away from his father's cottage darkness fell and he decided to spend the night in a roadside inn.

'Hey there,' shouted the travellers when they saw him come in. 'Come and sit with us, or there will soon be nothing left to eat!'

'I wouldn't dream of depriving you.' said the boy. 'On the contrary be my guests.'

So saying, he set the little table down in the middle of the room and said: 'Little table, lay yourself!' At once the most delicious dishes appeared on the table, their fragrance tickling the nostrils of the astonished guests.

'Take what you want,' said the young joiner. 'Eat as much as you like, friends!'

Once they had overcome their astonishment, the travellers set to with a will and however much they ate the dishes were always full again.

The innkeeper was keeping an eye on the extraordinary scene.

'Perhaps I had better take this young man on as my cook,' he thought. 'It wouldn't cost me a penny to feed my customers!'

The feasting went on until midnight, when the young man went up to his room, carrying the table, which he put down in a corner before falling into a deep sleep.

The innkeeper, however, was unable to sleep.

'If only I could get that table for myself,' he thought. 'Ah, I remember now, I have one just like it in my attic. It may not be a magic table, but it will serve me well nonetheless!'

He stole up to the attic at once, found his own table and silently put it in the place of the magic table.

The next morning the young man paid his bill and left the inn, carrying what he believed to be his magic table on his back.

He reached his father's house a little before noon and the old tailor welcomed him joyfully.

'I'm happy to see you, my son,' he said. 'What have you been doing all this time?'

'I have been learning to be be a joiner, father.'

'That's a good thing. But what have you got there? It's not a very interesting looking table!'

56

'Maybe, but it's a magic table. I have only to say: "Little table, lay yourself!" and it is immediately covered with the most delicious dishes. Let's invite our friends to dinner tonight.'

The tailor was pleased with the idea and that evening the young man pronounced the magic phrase – but the table remained as bare as any ordinary table. The joiner was in despair when he realized that someone had exchanged his magic table for an ordinary piece of furniture, and he was deeply ashamed to think that once again his father and friends would call him a liar.

The tailor had been hoping to retire when he heard of the magic table, but now he had to take up his needle again, whilst his eldest son found work with another joiner.

Now, the second son had found a position with a miller and when the time came for him to leave, his master said: 'I have nothing but praise for your work. As your reward, take this donkey. Although it can neither pull a cart nor carry a load, it will be very useful to you.'

'How is that?' asked the young man in surprise.

'All you have to do,' said his master, 'is to spread a cloth under its hoofs and say: "Donk, donk!" and gold coins will tumble from it, front and back!'

'I really am in luck,' said the boy and thanking his master he went off with the donkey.

After that his life was free from care, his purse was always well filled and after saying the magic words to his donkey he had only to gather up the coins.

'Perhaps I should return to my father,' he thought after a time. 'My donkey will make him forget his anger and he will welcome me home.'

He set off, but on the last night of his journey he decided to stop at the very same inn where his elder brother's table had been stolen.

'Tell me where to put my donkey, innkeeper,' said the young man. 'I will settle it in myself – my donkey is too precious to be left with anyone else.'

The innkeeper thought the traveller must be very poor to attach so much importance to a wretched donkey, but he changed his mind when he saw the two gold pieces which the young man held out to him, saying:

'Go and prepare your best dishes for me. I wish to dine well.'

After the meal, the miller asked if he owed the innkeeper anything more and the greedy man decided to demand two more pieces of gold.

'Just a minute, ' said the young man 'I will go and fetch some more money.'

Taking his cloth with him, he went to the stable and shut himself in, but the innkeeper had followed him stealthily and watched through the keyhole while his customer spread the cloth on the ground. Then he heard him say: 'Donk, donk!'

At once gold coins tumbled onto the cloth, both front and back.

'Bless my boots and saucepans!' muttered the innkeeper, 'That's an easy way to earn money!'

When the miller had paid his bill and gone to bed, the innkeeper slipped off to the stable and exchanged for the walking treasury an ordinary donkey which looked exactly like the other.

The next morning the boy went to the stable, collected the donkey and was soon at his father's cottage.

'Ah, so there you are, my son!' said the tailor. 'I am very glad to see you. What have you been doing all this time?'

'I have become a miller, father.'

'That's a good trade. Have you brought back some souvenir of your travels?'

'Only a donkey,' said the boy.

'We have no use for a donkey here,' said the tailor. 'A new goat would have been more useful.'

'To be sure,' said the miller, 'but this is no ordinary donkey. I have only to say: ''Donk, donk!'' and gold coins fall from it in front and behind. Invite all your friends in and I will make them rich!'

'The Lord be praised!' said the tailor. 'I shall be able to retire at last.'

When the party was assembled that evening the young miller spread his cloth on the ground and led his donkey onto it.

'Watch now!' he cried. And then he spoke the magic charm: 'Donk, donk!'

But nothing happened; not a piece of gold tumbled to the ground and the donkey was as deaf to the magic as any other donkey. The young miller realized that he had been robbed and with his face as long as a fiddle he had to apologise to their guests, who left as poor as they had arrived.

The tailor took up his needle again and the young man had to work for another miller.

What had been happening to the youngest son all this time? He had found work with a wood-turner. His was a craft which took longer to learn than those of his brothers, so his apprenticeship was a long one. He wrote to his brothers at home and they wrote back to tell him of their misfortune and how the inn-keeper had played a trick on them and stolen their magic treasures from them.

When the time came for the young turner to leave, his master, who valued him highly, presented him with a bag containing a hefty cudgel.

'Ah well, master,' said the boy, 'the bag will be useful and I will put it over my shoulder, but what is the point of this cudgel, which will only weigh it down?'

'The answer, my friend,' said the master turner, 'is that this is no ordinary cudgel. If anyone wishes you ill you have only to say : "Cudgel, out of my bag!" and the cudgel will give him such a beating that he will be laid low for a week, and it will not stop until you say: "Cudgel, into my bag!".'

The young man thanked his master and left with his bag over his shoulder. Whenever some awkward fellow annoyed him he would say: 'Cudgel, out of my bag!' and the cudgel would set to with a will, so that the young man's journey was made quite easy for him.

At last he arrived at that inn where his brothers had been robbed of their fortune. Sitting down at a table, he put his bag in front of him and started to talk about all the wonders he had seen on his travels.

'Of course, I've often seen magic tables tottering under the weight of food and donkeys that produced gold and other marvels. But all those are nothing to the treasure I have in my bag here!'

The innkeeper pricked up his ears.

'What can there be in that bag?' he wondered. 'Probably a whole pile of precious stones. I'll soon get my hands on it, mark my words – good things

always come in threes.'

The young man lay down on a bench to sleep, tucking the bag under his head as a pillow, and when the innkeeper thought he was sound alseep he tip-toed over to the bag, pulling gently at it by one corner.

The young turner, who had been expecting him, murmured under his breath: 'Cudgel, out of my bag!' At once the cudgel leaped from the bag and beat the innkeeper on his back and shoulders.

The innkeeper begged for mercy, but the more he yelled, the faster the cudgel worked, until he lay helpless on the ground.

'Give me back the magic table and the donkey that produces gold,' said the turner, 'otherwise my cudgel will be dancing on your back again!'

'Take them, take them for the love of heaven!' cried the innkeeper. 'Stop that cudgel of yours, I beg you!'

'Very well then. I will stop it, but mind you keep your word. Cudgel, into the bag!' he said, and off he went with the table and the donkey and his precious bag over his shoulder.

'What have you been doing all this time?' his father asked him.

'I have become a turner,' said the young man.

'That's a really good trade,' cried his father. 'You're a real artist! But what masterpiece have you brought back with you?'

'Something very precious,' said his son, ' a cudgel, in this bag.'

'What?' said his father, 'A cudgel! You could have cut one from any tree!'

'This is no ordinary cudgel,' said the young man. 'I have only to say: "Cudgel, out of my bag!" and it gives anyone who is bothering me a sound thrashing. Look, father, thanks to the cudgel I have brought my elder brother's magic table with me, and my second brother's donkey that produces gold. Call them, and call all our friends. We will feed them well and make them rich.'

This time the tailor hesitated, but the brothers persuaded him and soon the cottage was full of guests.

Now it was the young turner who spread the cloth on the ground, led the donkey onto it and said to his brother:

'Now, it is for you to speak.'

The miller said 'Donk, donk!' and at once the cloth was covered with gold. The donkey did not stop until everyone had as much as he wanted.

Then the turner set the little table in the middle of the room and said to his elder brother:

'Dear brother, now it is your turn.'

Scarcely had the joiner said: 'Little table, lay yourself,' when the table was covered with a great variety of dishes and delicious wines to drink. What a joyful feast that was!

At last the tailor could set aside his needle and thread, his ruler and iron and live happily with his three clever sons.

And what of the mischievous goat which caused all the trouble? That goat was very ashamed of its shaven head and hid in the first hole it came to. This turned out to be the lair of Reynard the fox and when the fox came home, the sight of two great yellow eyes in the darkness of his lair sent him running off in terror.

'Where are you running to?' called Bruin the bear. 'You look as if the devil were on your heels.'

'Oh, my friend,' said the fox, 'I can never go home again. There is a monster in my lair and I would never dare to chase it out.'

'We'll go together,' said the bear, but no sooner did they reach the lair than he too started back at the sight of the goat's blazing eyes.

'Where are you running to?' asked the bee. 'You look as if you're in a terrible hurry!'

'There's a dreadful animal in Reynard's lair and we don't know how to get it out!'

'You stupid beasts,' said the bee, 'I am only a tiny insect, but I'll deal with it for you.'

Off she flew to the fox's lair, where she stung the shaven head of the goat so hard that the goat took flight, bleating with pain, and as far as I know it has never been seen again.

KING
THRUSHBEARD

There was once a king who had a very beautiful daughter, but she was so proud and vain that he could not persuade her to marry. No suitor was good enough for her; she made fun of them all and sent them packing.

One day the king gave a feast to which he invited all the likely lords and rulers who might seek his daughter's hand.

'Built like a battleship!' she laughed in the face of a broad-shouldered, thick-set king. 'A matchstick!' she tittered, at the sight of a very tall, very thin duke. 'Quite a little barrel!' she mocked a short prince with a slight pot-belly. 'White as a sheet!' (this prince was very pale) 'Look, a poppy!' (a red-faced prince) and 'Unripe but withered!' she scoffed at a young lord with a wrinkled face.

But her sharpest sarcasm was kept for an unfortunate king at the very end of the line, who had a rather pointed chin.

'Just look at that chin!' she sniggered. 'Doesn't it remind you of a thrush's beak?' From that moment on the king was known as Thrushbeard.

The princess's father flew into a rage at his daughter's rudeness.

'You shall marry the first beggar who presents himself at the palace gates!' he told her.

Two days later, a poor musician was heard singing outside the window.

'Bring him in,' said the king, and in came a ragged, dusty man, who sang for them and then begged for alms.

'Instead of alms, you shall have my daughter,' said the king, and in spite of the princess's tears and pleading, he called a priest to celebrate the marriage at once.

'Now you must go,' said the king. 'A palace is no place for a beggar's wife.'

No carriage, either, for the proud princess, who had to follow her husband on foot until they reached a great forest.

'Ah!' wept the princess:

> *'Whose is this forest that I see?*
> *Is it not Thrushbeard's home?*
> *Would that this place belonged to me—*
> *No longer would I roam!'*

On the other side of the forest they entered a green meadow. The princess wept again:

> *'Whose is the meadow that I see?*
> *Is it not Thrushbeard's home?*
> *Would that this place belonged to me—*
> *No longer would I roam!'*

After this, they walked through a great town, and once again the princess sobbed:

> *'Whose is this city that I see?*
> *Is it not Thrushbeard's home?*
> *Would that this place belonged to me —*
> *No longer would I roam!'*

'I've had enough of your whining!' growled the beggar. 'You can stop wishing for another man's goods and make do with mine!'

At last they stopped at a miserable hut.

'Oh Lord, Lord,' moaned the princess, 'who could live in such a place?'

'You and me!' said the beggar.

'Where are the servants?' said the princess.

'What servants?' retorted the beggar. 'You'll do the work yourself. Get the fire lit, put some water on and cook the dinner. I'm tired and hungry.'

Of course the princess had no idea what to do, so the meal was poor and they went hungry to their hard bed. The princess seemed scarcely to have slept at all when her husband roused her to do the housework. After only a few days there was no more food in the house.

'Wife,' said the beggar, 'we need money. You must weave some baskets and sell them in the market-place.'

He cut some willow wands and brought them to the princess, who tried to weave them together, but only succeeded in tearing her fingers.

'I can see you're no good at making baskets,' said the beggar. 'I'll get some flax – perhaps spinning will suit you better.'

The girl set to work, but the coarse thread cut her hands, which were soon covered with blood.

'I made a bad bargain, marrying you,' said the beggar. 'You're good for nothing. Tomorrow I'll fetch some pots for you to take to market. You'll have to do nothing but sell them.'

'Alas,' said the princess, 'if any of my father's subjects should pass by, how they would laugh at me!'

But she had to obey, and for the sake of her pretty face people bought the pots at a good price.

When the money she had earned ran out, the beggar bought a second load of pots and his wife went out again to sell them. She chose a spot at the corner of a road and was arranging her goods about her, when a horseman came galloping straight towards her and his horse's flying hoofs smashed her pots to smithereens.

'What am I to do?' moaned the princess. 'What will my husband say?'

When she had told her story, the beggar burst out: 'No one in her senses would try to sell pottery on a street corner! It seems you're unable to do anything right. I'm going to ask if they'll take you on as kitchen maid at our king's palace, for your keep.'

So the princess became a kitchen maid. In return for the lowliest tasks, she was given the left-overs from the royal table, and these she put in two pots until evening, when she and her husband shared them in their hut.

One day there was great excitement in the palace. The king was to be married, and everyone, even the little kitchen maid, went up to the great hall to peep round the door at the celebrations.

When all the flares were lighted and the guests were arriving, magnificently dressed, the princess thought sadly of her wretched fate and the pride and vanity which had brought her so low. Kindly servants gave the weeping girl many morsels of the delicious dishes served for the feast, and she put them in the two little pots in her apron to take home.

Suddenly the king himself appeared, in a dazzling suit of silk and velvet, with a heavy gold chain about his neck. When he saw the pretty maid in the doorway, he took her hand and tried to make her dance with him, but the princess twisted and turned, trembling with fear because she had recognized in him King Thrushbeard, whom she had once mocked.

But the king would not let go of her hand and in a moment she was in the centre of the great hall. Unfortunately the strings of her apron had come loose as she struggled and the two pots containing all her morsels of food fell to the floor and broke in pieces. There was a roar of laughter from the assembled company and the humiliated princess fled towards the kitchen.

Her way was barred again by King Thrushbeard.

'Have no fear,' he said gently, 'the beggar whose life you have shared and the king who stands before you now are one and the same. I was also the horseman who broke your pots. I did all these things for love of you, to break your foolish pride!'

The princess burst into tears. 'I did wrong, very wrong,' she sobbed. 'I am not worthy to be your wife.'

'You are now,' said the king firmly. 'Your time of trial is over and we can be married at last.'

The princess was hurried off by ladies-in-waiting and reappeared soon afterwards, clothed like a queen.

And the happiest of all the guests at the wedding was her old father, who had helped to bring about a marriage of true love at last.

SNOW WHITE AND ROSE-RED

There was once a poor widow who lived alone with her two daughters in a cottage surrounded by a small garden in which two rose trees grew. The roses on one were white, on the other red and the two little girls had skins as fresh and clear as rose petals and because one had the fairest of fair hair and the other wonderful auburn locks, their mother called them Snow-White and Rose-Red.

Snow-White was a calm and gentle girl, but Rose-Red loved to run across the fields, picking flowers and surprising the birds on their nests. Meanwhile, Snow-White would happily help her mother in her household tasks and sit down beside her to read aloud when all their work was done.

The two sisters loved one another dearly.

'We shall never be parted,' said Snow-White.

'No, never, as long as we live,' said Rose-Red.

'Always be sure to share everything you have,' said their mother.

When the two girls went walking in the forest, no animal ever feared or harmed them. The hare nibbled cabbage leaves from their hands, the roe-deer grazed at their feet, the stag leaped joyfully about them and the birds in the trees sang for them alone. They could even spend the whole night there, sleeping on the moss, without fear.

One morning, after a peaceful night in the forest, they woke up at sunrise to see a pretty child sitting beside them, dressed all in white. Smiling sweetly at the girls, the child rose to his feet and walked off into the forest without a word. It was then that Snow-White and Rose-Red discovered that they had been sleeping on the brink of a precipice.

They ran home to their mother and told their story.

'The child was your guardian angel,' she told them. 'They watch over all good children!'

The two girls kept the cottage neat and clean all the year round. In summer Red-Rose saw to the housework, and every morning, before her mother was awake, she placed one red rose and one white in a bowl at the foot of her mother's bed. In winter Snow-White lit the fire early and hung the cooking pot over it to boil. It was only a copper pot, but she made it shine like gold.

One winter evening, when the snow was falling thickly, Snow-White had bolted the door and the little family was sitting before the fire, the two girls spinning while their mother read aloud to them. A woolly lamb lay at their feet and a turtle-dove slept on a perch behind them.

Suddenly they heard a knock at the door.

'Open the door quickly, Rose-Red,' said her mother. 'Some poor traveller needs shelter from the cold.'

When Rose-Red opened the door she saw no benighted traveller but a brown bear, whose great frame filled the doorway. Rose-Red cried out and jumped back from the door, the lamb bleated, the turtle-dove flapped its wings and Snow-White hid behind their mother's bed.

'Have no fear,' said the bear softly, 'I shall not harm you. I am half dead with cold and have come to beg a little warmth at your hearth.'

'Come in, poor creature,' said the mother, 'and take care not to singe your beautiful fur at the fireside.'

Then she called her daughters:

'Snow-White! Rose-Red! Come back now. The bear has promised that no harm will come to us.'

The bear sank down before the fire, growling with pleasure.

'Kind children,' he said, 'will you brush the snow from my fur?'

After doing as he asked, the girls felt quite at home with the great beast, thrusting their little hands into his thick coat and tickling him with a hazel twig. The bear growled, the girl laughed with delight, but when their play became too rough, he begged them:

'Gently, little ones! Snow-White, Rose-Red, you wouldn't want to kill a poor wild animal, would you?'

When bed-time came, the mother spoke kindly to the bear:

'In God's name, stay where you are, safe from the cold and snow.'

After that the bear came to sleep in the cottage every night and played in the forest with the girls by day, but when spring came, bringing back the green leaves, he told Snow-White:

'I have to leave you now, and I shall not return all summer long.'

'Where are you going, dear Bear?' Snow-White asked.

'I must return to the forest to guard my treasures, which the wicked dwarfs would like to steal from me. In wintertime the ground is frozen hard and they do not leave their underground caverns, but as soon as the earth softens in the spring, they come out again, thieving and pilfering, and what they have taken is never seen again.'

Snow-White was sad to see her big friend go, but as he walked out of the door a tuft of his fur caught on a nail and she was quite sure that she saw a flash of gold beneath it.

A few days later, the sisters were sent to the forest to gather wood. Coming to a fallen tree, they saw something strange bobbing up and down behind it. Running round to look, they found a wrinkled dwarf, with his long beard caught in a crack. He was leaping to and fro like a chained dog, trying to free himself.

'What do you think you're doing , staring at me like a couple of blockheads? Come and get me out of here at once!'

'How did it happen, little man?' asked Rose-Red.

'Curiosity killed the cat,' snapped the dwarf. 'I was lopping the tree for some little logs. I needed them to cook our little dishes. We can't use big branches like you, because we don't guzzle like you, you great gluttons! I had driven my wedge in here, but the wretched wood is too springy, the wedge shot out and the crack closed on my beautiful white beard. Now get me out!'

The young girls were sympathetic, as always, but they could not help smiling at the sight of the angry dwarf, leaping about and shouting.

'So you'd laugh at me, would you, you plucked chickens!' he shrieked. 'I never saw such ugly faces!'

'I'll run for help,' said Rose-Red at once.

'Silly donkey!' retorted the dwarf. 'Two of you is two too many. Think again!'

'I've had another idea,' said Snow-White, and from her pocket she took a small pair of scissors with which she cut off the tip of the dwarf's beard.

As soon as he was free, the dwarf snatched up a bag of gold which had been hidden among the roots of the tree and ran off with it, screaming:

'How dare you cut my beard! You'll get no thanks from me!'

A few days later the sister went out to catch a fish for supper, but as they approached the stream they could see something like a big grasshopper jumping up and down, almost falling in the river. In a moment they saw that it was the dwarf.

'Where are you off to?' asked Rose-Red. 'You surely don't mean to go for a swim?'

'I'm not as stupid as you are!' shouted the dwarf. 'Can't you see that wretched fish, trying to drown me?'

The little man had settled down to fish when his beard became tangled in his line and a big fish, taking the bait, had almost pulled the weak little creature into the river with him.

The sisters had arrived just in time, but try as they might, they could not disentangle the beard from the fishing line. In the end they had no alternative but to cut the dwarf's beard again.

When he realized that he had lost a few more inches of beard, the dwarf positively shook with fury.

'I suppose you like going round disfiguring people, you silly geese?' he yelled. 'You can go to the devil, and may your shoes lose their soles!'

Soon afterwards, the sisters were walking to the village to buy needles and thread, when they saw a great eagle circling over a rock. Just as it landed they heard a scream of terror and when they ran to the spot they found that it was gripping in its claws their old acquaintance, the bad-tempered dwarf.

They seized the dwarf's beard and pulled with all their strength, until the eagle released its prey.

'Can't you ever do anything right?' screamed the dwarf. 'You pulled so hard that the eagle's claws have torn off half my coat! You're nothing but a pair of clumsy good-for-nothings!'

By now the girls were quite used to his ingratitude and they walked on and did their shopping as if nothing had happened. On the way home, they saw the dwarf once more, but this time he was gloating over the contents of his bag, a heap of precious stones, sparkling like flames in the light of the setting sun.

'What do you think you're doing, with your fried-fish eyes?' he shrieked when he caught sight of them, hoping that his insults would make them run away. But at that moment they heard a deep growl, and a bear came out of the trees at a fast trot. The terrified dwarf had no time to run, so he fell on his knees:

'My lord Bear,' he sobbed, 'spare me! I will give you all my treasure – just look at these pretty stones! I'm not worth eating – why don't you take those

two little girls, as plump as partridges? You could really sink your teeth in them!'

The bear ignored his pleas and felled the little man with one stroke of his great paw, while the two girls ran off as fast as they could. But the bear called them back:

'Snow-White! Rose-Red! Don't be afraid – wait for me!'

Then they recognised their friend's voice and stopped. As the bear reached them, his furry coat dropped to the ground and a handsome young man stood before them, clothed in gold from head to foot.

'I am a king's son,' he told them, 'and I was put under a spell by that wicked dwarf who stole my treasure. Only his death could set me free, and now at long last he has received the punishment he deserved.'

It was not long before the prince married Snow-White, while Rose-Red became his brother's bride, sharing the vast treasure which the dwarf had amassed in his cave.

The widowed mother lived on for many happy years with her daughters, keeping at her door the two rose trees which she had brought from their humble cottage.

And every year, as soon as it was spring, the two trees were covered with beautiful roses, white and red.

THE ELVES
AND THE
SHOEMAKER

Once there was an honest shoemaker and his wife who were very poor. They were so poor that they had only enough leather left to make one pair of shoes.

So one evening, the shoemaker cut out his last pair of shoes, laid the pieces on his bench, said his prayers like the good man he was, and went to bed.

The next morning, when he entered his workshop, the prettiest pair of shoes he had ever seen was standing on the bench.

The shoemaker was still staring at them when a customer came in, saw the exquisite shoes and bought them on the spot.

Now the shoemaker had enough money to buy leather for two pairs of shoes, which he cut out and left on the bench. The next morning, two perfect pairs of shoes were waiting for him. Once again, the beautiful shoes found ready buyers and the good shoemaker had enough money for leather to cut out four more pairs. And once again, the shoes were ready when he came down next morning.

Soon the shoemaker was making a good living again and his wife was able to buy everything they needed. She shared her husband's surprise and pleasure, but one night, just before Christmas, she thought they should find out who was helping them. Her husband agreed and together they hid behind a curtain, prepared to wait all night if necessary.

Just as the clock struck twelve, the door opened and in came two little elves as naked as they were nimble.

In a moment they were at the cobbler's bench, punching holes in the shaped pieces of leather and sewing them together so skilfully with their tiny fingers that the shoemaker and his wife gaped in astonishment. Only when all the leather had been turned into shoes did they skip away.

'Husband,' said the shoemaker's wife, 'those little elves have saved us from ruin – let's show them how grateful we are! I'm going to make each of them a little shirt and a doublet and hose, and I shall knit a tiny pair of stockings for them both.'

'And I shall make them each a fine pair of shoes,' her husband added.

On Christmas Eve the little sets of clothes were ready, and the shoemaker and his wife laid them out carefully on the bench, where the pieces of leather were usually left at night.

Then they hid in the corner as before and waited to see what would happen.

At midnight the elves came hopping in, all ready to start work, but instead of shoe leather, they found the little suits. For a moment the little people were quite startled. Then they began to jump for joy, and putting on their new clothes they danced round and round, singing:

We are so fine and gaily dressed,
We'll give our cobbling work a rest!

On and on they danced, over the work-bench, on the seat and round the room, and when they went out of the door they were still dancing.

They were never seen again from that day on. But the shoemaker's business prospered for the rest of his life and he died a happy and successful man.

LUCKY
HANS

H ans had served his master loyally for seven years. One morning he said: 'It's time for me to go home to my mother.'

'You have been honest and hardworking, and I wish to reward you,' said his master. 'Here is a lump of gold for you, you have earned it!'

Hans thanked him, took the gold – a lump the size of his head – wrapped it carefully in his bundle, slung the bundle over his shoulder and strode away.

Hans had been walking for quite a long time when a horseman passed him at a brisk trot.

'Oho!' cried Hans, 'what fun it must be to ride – no stones to hurt your feet, you save shoe-leather and you get there as comfortably as if you were sitting in an armchair.'

The horseman stopped. 'Why go on foot, then?'

'What else can I do?' said Hans. 'I'm going home after seven years with my master, and I'm carrying such a load that I can't straighten my back. It's a lump of gold, you see.'

'Simple!' said the horseman, 'let's exchange my horse for your gold.'

'Wonderful,' said Hans, 'but you'll have your work cut out carrying it, I promise you!'

'I'll give you a leg up,' said the horseman, dismounting very quickly. 'If you want to go faster, click your tongue and shout Gee-up! Gee-up!'

Hans enjoyed the ride at first, but he was soon tired of going so slowly. 'Gee-up! Gee-up!' he cried, clicking his tongue. The horse leaped forward and poor Hans found himself at the bottom of the ditch, while the horse cantered on.

Fortunately a farmer taking his cow to market caught the horse by the bridle, while Hans rose painfully to his feet.

'That's the last time I ride a horse,' he groaned. 'That cow of yours, now – there's a peaceful beast for you! And there's your daily ration of milk, butter and cheese as well. What wouldn't I give for an animal like that!'

'Well, if that's what you want,' said the farmer, 'let's exchange my cow for your horse!'

'With all my heart,' said Hans. The farmer handed over the cow's tether, bounded on to the horse's back and made off at high speed.

Hans strolled along beside his cow. 'When I'm hungry,' he rejoiced, 'I have only to cut a slice of bread and spread butter and cheese on it. And when I'm thirsty I have only to milk my cow and drink the milk. What more could I ask?'

Much later in the morning Hans reached an inn, where he decided to stop.

'I can let myself go now,' he thought. 'I have food and drink of my own in plenty.'

So saying, he ate up all his provisions and spent his last few pence on a pint of beer.

Then he set off again with his cow on the long road to his mother's village. The day grew very warm, there was no shade to be found, and the poor boy became so hot and thirsty that his tongue stuck to the roof of his mouth.

'It's time to milk my cow,' he said, 'then I can quench my thirst.'

Tethering the cow to a stump, and using his hat in place of a pail, he began to squeeze the cow's udders, but he was so clumsy that the cow lashed out with both back legs and sent poor Hans tumbling in the dust.

'What a to-do!' cried a butcher who was wheeling a piglet along in a wheelbarrow. Hans told his story and the good man handed him his water bottle.

'Have a drink, friend,' he said. 'As for that cow, you'll not get another drop of milk from her, believe me! She's only fit to be sold for meat.'

'Who would have thought it?' muttered Hans, scratching his head. 'A cow is quite a mouthful, to be sure, but I'm not too keen on cow's meat myself. Your piglet, now – there's a tasty morsel, if ever there was one! And as for the sausages . . .'

'Hark 'ee, lad,' said the butcher, 'we could make an exchange: my pig for your cow.'

'God bless your kind heart!' cried Hans, and handing over the cow to the butcher, he tied a rope round the pig's neck and walked off, thinking happily of all the good luck he had been having. No sooner did a problem arise than it was solved!

He was overtaken soon afterwards by a boy carrying a fine fat goose. As they walked along together, Hans told his companion how well all his exchanges had worked out and the boy told him that the goose was to be the main dish at a christening party in the next village.

'Feel the weight,' he told Hans. 'They've been feeding her up for two months. Bite into that when she's roasted and you'll have fat right out of your ears!'

'She's a good weight,' Hans agreed, 'but my pig's not so bad, either.'

The boy darted a glance to right and left.

'Listen,' he whispered, 'about this pig of yours – there was one missing from the mayor's piggery in the last village and I'm very much afraid it's this one! The police are after the thief now and you'll be in trouble if they catch you – better hide somewhere, and quickly.'

Poor Hans was terrified. 'What am I to do?' he cried piteously. 'You know the country better than I do – how about giving me a hand? Take my pig and give me your goose!'

'You're asking me to run a risk,' said the boy, 'but I wouldn't want to leave you in a hole.' And he picked up the pig's rope and ran off with it down a side-road.

Greatly relieved, Hans picked up the goose and set out once more.

'I came out of that well after all,' he said to himself. 'Here's a fine roast, and enough fat for three months' cooking into the bargain, not to speak of the white down I shall have left for a soft pillow! Won't my mother be pleased!'

There was one village left before he reached home, and there he met a knife-grinder working his wheel. As he worked, he sang:

> Scissors and knives I grind,
> Turn swiftly, turn, my wheel!
> Ever in peace of mind,
> Turn swiftly, turn, my wheel!
> Fortune and fate are kind,
> Turn swiftly, turn, my wheel!

Hans stopped. 'Things seem to be going well for you,' he said as he watched.

'Yes, indeed,' said the knife-grinder. 'If you work with your hands, you've got a gold-mine. How about you? Where did you get that fine goose?'

'I exchanged it for a pig,' said Hans.

'And the pig?'

'I got it in exchange for a cow.'

'And the cow?'

'In exchange for a horse.'

'And the horse?'

'In exchange for a lump of gold as big as my head.'

'And the gold?'

'That was my wage for seven years' work!'

'You did well every time,' said the knife-grinder. 'And if this time you finish up with money in your pocket for life, you can be well pleased.'

'But how?' said Hans.

'Become a knife-grinder like me! All you need to start with is a grindstone, and the rest will follow. I've got one here that's a bit worn, but I wouldn't mind exchanging it for your goose. Do you want it?'

'You bet!' Hans exclaimed. 'What more could I ask? I shall soon be the happiest man on earth, because every time I put my hand in my pocket I'll find it full of tinkling brass.'

Into the knife-grinder's waiting arms went the goose and into Hans's hands went the grindstone.

'And here's another,' added the knife-grinder, picking up an even more worn stone. 'You could use it for all kinds of things, like straightening bent nails.'

'My word!' cried the delighted Hans, 'I must be the luckiest chap in the world.'

Hans was quite tired after his long walk, however, and now he was weighed down by the two big stones. Catching sight of a sparkling spring, he decided to rest a while and quench his thirst. He set down his stones on the brink of the spring, but as he stopped he made a clumsy movement and the two stones went rolling into the water. As he saw them go, Hans jumped for joy, then fell on his knees and thanked the good Lord for relieving him of his heavy burden without even being asked. Lightened in heart and body, he ran rejoicing to his mother's house.

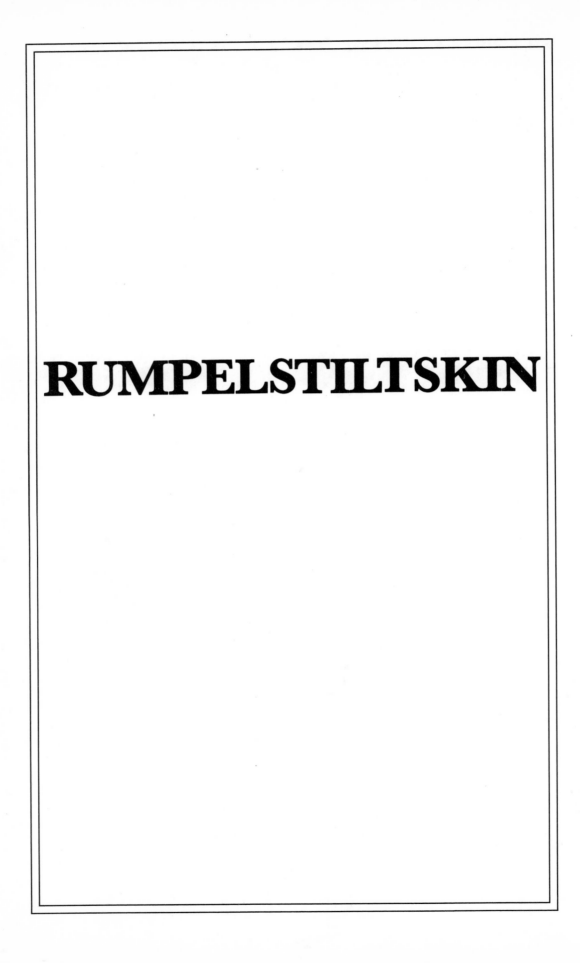

RUMPELSTILTSKIN

There was once a poor miller whose only treasure was his beautiful daughter. The miller was always boasting about her, even claiming powers for her which she did not possess.

One day, chancing to be in the king's presence, he claimed that his daughter could spin gold from straw. 'Why did I say it?' he muttered, a moment after, but it was too late.

'Bring me your daughter tomorrow,' ordered the king, who was looking forward to filling his treasury without lifting a finger.

The miller could only obey, and the next day his trembling daughter arrived at the palace. The king led her to a room piled high with straw.

'Here are wheel and spindle,' he told her. 'To work! And if this straw is not all transformed into gold by dawn, you will die!'

Left alone, the poor child sat down on a stool and gazed in horror at the mass of straw which she had to turn into gold. The more she thought about it, the less she could imagine how to do it. Despair overwhelmed her and she began to cry – but as the first tears fell, the door opened and a strange little man walked in.

'Why are you crying, little miller's girl?' he asked.

'Alas,' the girl sobbed, 'I must die tomorrow unless I can turn all this straw into gold!'

'What will you give me if I spin it for you?' asked the dwarf.

'I will give you my necklace,' said the girl.

The little man took the necklace, sat down on the stool, grasped the spindle, turned the wheel, and in only a few seconds he had filled two bobbins with golden thread.

At daybreak the king came in and saw the gold that had been spun from straw. Now, the king was so greedy that his pleasure lasted for no more than a blink – then he wanted more.

That evening, after the miller's daughter had rested, he led her to a much bigger room, in which there was even more straw.

'If life is dear to you,' he told her, 'turn all this straw into gold by morning!'

The girl did her best, but her clumsy thread was far from golden. She burst into tears and at once the dwarf appeared.

'What will you give me if I spin it for you?' he asked.

'I will give you the ring on my finger,' said the girl.

The little man took the ring, sat down on the stool, grasped the spindle, turned the wheel and began to spin. By morning all the straw had been turned into shining golden thread.

The king was dizzy with joy, but still he wanted more. That very evening, he led the poor girl to a room as big as a ballroom, piled to the ceiling with straw.

'This is your final test,' said the king. 'You will turn all this straw to gold, or you will not leave this place alive. But if you succeed, you shall be my queen!'

As before, when the miller's daughter was alone, the dwarf appeared.

'What will you give me if I spin it for you?' he asked again.

'I have no more to give,' said the girl.

'Then promise me your first child, when you are queen.'

The miller's daughter had no choice, if she wanted to stay alive, and once again the dwarf grasped the spindle, spun the wheel and by morning all the straw had been turned to gold.

Satisfied at last, the king gave orders for the marriage feast. A few days later, the miller's daughter was his queen.

A year passed and the queen gave birth to a son. Resting alone in her room, she saw a little man walk in without knocking.

'I have come to take what you promised,' said the dwarf.

The poor queen, who had forgotten all about him, promised him all the treasures of the kingdom if he would leave her son, but the dwarf refused.

The queen was heartbroken and at last her tears made him relent a little.

'I will give you three days,' he said, 'and if you can tell me my name in that time, you may keep your son.'

The queen spent the night recording every name she could remember and in the morning she sent out three messengers to find more names.

When the dwarf arrived that evening she told him all the names she had thought of and all those that the first messenger had found. But to all of them the dwarf said only:

'That's not my name!'

Next day the second messenger returned from his long journey and told the queen all the extraordinary names he had found.

'Is your name Leg-of-Lamb, Shoe-Lace or Cow's Horn?' the queen asked the dwarf.

But to each he said only:

'That's not my name!'

On the third day the last messenger returned with his story.

'I came on the second day to a dense forest which is not like other forests. The hare keeps company with the fox there and the trees have the strangest shapes you can imagine. In a clearing I saw a little man dancing round a fire and singing:

Today I knead, tomorrow I bake,
Next day the royal prince I'll take.
For never will they guess my game:
Rumpelstiltskin is my name!

The queen's heart bounded with joy and when the dwarf arrived that evening he was surprised to find her so cheerful.

'Well,' he snapped, 'do you know my name?'

'Is it Ludovic?'

'No.'

'Is it Ambrose?'

'That is not my name!'

'I suppose,' she said, smiling at him, 'it could not possibly be Rumpelstiltskin?'

'By all the imps in hell,' he cried, 'it was the devil himself who told you that!'

In his rage the dwarf stamped his foot so violently that his leg went through the floor and as he continued to thrash about he sank deeper and deeper, until the earth closed over him and he vanished from sight. No one has ever seen him since.

CLEVER ELSIE

A farmer and his wife had a daughter so intelligent that they called her Clever Elsie.

'It's time she married,' said her father one day.

'If we can find someone to marry her,' said her mother.

At last they found a boy called John, who lived quite a long way off.

'I will marry her, if she's as intelligent as you say,' he promised.

Her parents invited John to supper, to meet Elsie.

'Run down to the cellar and draw some beer,' her mother told her. 'We don't want to run out.'

Clever Elsie took the pitcher down to the cellar and set a stool before the barrel, to sit on while she drew the beer.

While the pitcher was filling up, Clever Elsie caught sight of a pickaxe hanging on the wall where the masons had left it. 'If I marry John,' cried poor Elsie, 'we shall have a son and when he grows up we shall send him down to the cellar for beer and the pickaxe will fall on his head and kill him!'

'What has happened to Elsie?' her mother wondered. 'Go down to the cellar,' she told the servant girl, 'and have a look!'

The servant girl found Elsie still sitting on her stool, her tears running faster than the beer.

'Why are you crying, Elsie?' the girl asked.

'I've got something to cry about,' sobbed Elsie. 'If I marry John, we shall have a son and when he grows up we shall send him down to the cellar for beer and that pickaxe will fall on his head and kill him!'

'Oh dearie me!' cried the girl. 'What a clever Elsie we've got!' And she sat down and cried.

'What has happened to Elsie?' asked her father impatiently. 'Go down to the cellar,' he told the manservant, 'and have a look!'

The man went down and found the two girls weeping.

'What are you crying for?' he asked them.

'I've got something to cry about,' sobbed Elsie. 'If I marry John, we shall have a son and when he grows up we shall send him down to the cellar for beer and that pickaxe will fall on his head and kill him!'

'By George!' cried the man. 'What a clever Elsie we've got!' And he sat down and cried.

'What has happened to Elsie?' grumbled her father. 'Go down to the cellar, wife, and have a look!'

His wife went down and found Elsie, the maid and the man sitting on their little stools, crying.

'Why are you crying?' she asked.

When Elsie explained that after marrying John she would have a child who was certain to be killed by the pickaxe in the cellar, her mother cried:

'Oh, what a clever Elsie we've got!' And she too sat down and cried.

By now the farmer was really thirsty. 'I'll have to go down to the cellar myself and have a look,' he told John.

When he saw them all crying and asked what was wrong, and when he heard that after marrying John, Elsie would have a child, who would grow up and go down to the cellar, where he would be killed by the mason's pickaxe, her father cried: 'Oh, what a clever Elsie we've got!' And he sat and began to cry with the others.

John sat upstairs alone for a long time, waiting. Then at last: 'They must be waiting for me downstairs,' he said. 'I must go and have a look.'

In the cellar he found them all crying and grieving for all they were worth.

'What's happened to you?' he asked.

'Oh, my dear John,' cried Elsie, 'when we're married, we shall have a son, he will grow up, we shall send him down to the cellar one day for beer and the pickaxe the masons have left will fall on his head and kill him! Isn't that worth crying about?'

'By heavens!' John exclaimed, 'you really are as intelligent as I hoped. I will marry you.'

They were married the same day.

One morning, John told his wife: 'I am off to work now and I would like you to go and cut some corn while I'm out. We're short of bread.'

'Certainly, my dear John,' said Elsie, and as soon as he had gone she went down to the field.

'Shall I cut the corn first, or shall I eat my snack?' she thought. 'I think I shall eat first.'

When she had eaten, she began to wonder again:

'Shall I cut the corn now, or shall I have a little rest? I think I'll have a little rest.'

And she lay down among the cornstalks and slept.

When evening came John went home, but there was no sign of his wife. 'She's still at work,' he thought, 'what a clever Elsie she is!'

After a while he thought he would go and find out how much corn she had cut, but when he reached the field he found the corn untouched and Elsie lying among the cornstalks, fast asleep.

John ran home and found the fowler's net, covered with little bells, which he used to catch birds. He ran to the field, threw it over Elsie, ran home again, shut the door and set to work.

When Elsie woke up the night was dark, and after she had struggled to her feet the bells rang at every step she took. 'Who am I?' the worried girl asked herself. 'Am I Clever Elsie, or not?' But as usual, she found it difficult to make up her mind.

'I know,' she said at last, 'I shall go home and ask John who I am!'

But when she got home, the door was shut.

'John!' she called. 'John! Is Elsie in there?'

'Yes, she's here,' said John.

Poor Elsie began to quake with fear. She ran to the house next door, but the sound of the bells made the neighbours suspicious and no one would take her in. So Clever Elsie left the village that night and was never seen again.

THE GOOSE GIRL AT THE SPRING

Once upon a time there was a little old woman – so old that it was impossible to guess her age – who lived all alone on a mountainside, above the trees. Her cottage lay in the midst of fields, where she kept her geese. Every morning she hobbled down to the forest with her crutch, but she worked much harder than you would have expected of one so old. She picked all the fruit she could reach and gathered sweet grass for her geese. When she met anyone, she would greet him cheerfully.

'Good day to you! Fine day!' Then she would go on: 'You may be surprised to see me carrying so much at my age, but people should bear their own burdens, don't you agree?'

All the same, most people tried to avoid the little old woman and mothers told their children not to talk to her – she might be a witch!

One morning a handsome young man walked whistling through the forest. The sun was shining, the birds were singing and a gentle breeze stirred the leaves. He had not seen a living soul until he came across the old woman kneeling on the ground, cutting grass with a sickle. She already had two basket-loads of wild apples and pears.

'Hello, mother!' cried the young man. 'How will you carry all that?'

'I have to look after myself,' she said. 'The rich can buy help, but we poor folk have to bear our own burdens. I won't refuse a helping hand, though – not from such as you, with your straight back and strong legs! I don't live far away – just the other side of that mountain. It won't take you long.'

The young man felt sorry for her. 'It's my good luck that I'm not a peasant but a rich nobleman's son,' he said. 'I'll help you. Never let it be said that the peasants have to bear their burdens alone.'

'Thank you,' said the old woman. 'You can walk it in an hour.'

The young man was not quite so pleased at the thought of an hour's walk, but before he could speak, she had put the sack of grass on his back and pushed the two baskets of fruit into his hands.

'You see,' she said, 'it's not as heavy as all that!'

'It's heavier,' he said. 'The sack on my shoulders feels as if it's stuffed with pebbles and the baskets pull on my arms like lead!'

The old woman laughed delightedly.

'You young people,' she cackled, 'you're all the same! You don't want to carry the loads I've been lugging about – you're all words, but when it comes to deeds ...! Come on now, get going. You're not going to throw off that burden!'

On level ground he could just manage, but as soon as they started climbing, with the stones slipping under his feet, it was past bearing. His face was beaded with sweat, his back was soaked.

'I can't go on, mother,' he panted. 'Let me rest a minute.'

'Not yet,' said the old woman. 'You can rest when we get there. It may not turn out too badly for you.'

'Now you're being cheeky, mother,' said the young nobleman. He tried to throw off his load, but the sack seemed to be stuck to his back like glue.

The old woman cackled again to see him twist and turn. 'Don't get upset, my friend,' she said. 'You're as red as a cock's comb. Be patient and you shall have your reward.'

The young man had no choice: he dragged himself painfully behind the old woman, who seemed to grow more and more agile, while his load grew heavier and heavier. Suddenly the old crone leaped on to the young man's shoulders, where in spite of her withered form, she weighed more heavily than the fat woman in the circus.

He could scarcely drag one foot past the other, but the crone had no pity. She used a switch on his shoulders and nettles on his legs. He was trembling like a jelly when he reached the cottage and almost collapsed on the threshold.

The geese came running to meet the crone, flapping their wings and calling. Behind them came a dreadful hag, her face as repulsive as the night, but she was tall and proud in her bearing.

'You've been gone a long time, mother,' she said. 'Is anything wrong?'

'Nothing at all,' said her mother. 'This charming young man carried all my things and even made me ride piggyback when he saw that I was tired. We had such a jolly chat on the way!'

So saying, the crone jumped down, took the young man's load off his back and gave him a smile.

'Sit down and rest now,' she said. 'Your reward will not be long in coming. And you,' she said to the goose-girl, 'come away! You mustn't be left alone with a young man – never play with fire! He might fall in love with you.'

The young nobleman did not know whether to laugh or cry.

'That little treasure!' he thought. 'If she were thirty years younger I'd still be in no danger.'

With a last caress for her geese, the crone went into the cottage with her daughter.

The young man stretched out in the shade. The air was warm and mild, the meadows dotted with primroses, buttercups and a thousand other flowers. A brook sparkled in the sunlight and the geese came and went, enjoying the sweet grass and clear water.

'This is a most delightful spot,' said the young man, 'but I'm so tired. If I don't sleep, I may fall to pieces!'

The old woman let him sleep for a time, then came out and woke him up.

'Get up,' she told him. 'You can't stay here. You have certainly toiled, but it hasn't killed you and I am going to reward you, though not with riches.'

She pressed into his hand a little box carved from an emerald.

'Guard it carefully,' she said. 'It will bring you happiness.'

The young nobleman thanked her warmly and said goodbye, without even glancing at the hideous hag.

After walking for three days he reached an unfamiliar town. As a stranger, he was taken to the palace and presented to the king and queen, whom he honoured with the gift of the emerald box. The queen thanked him, opened the box and swooned away. The guards seized the young man, but when she came to her senses again, the queen told them to let him go.

'Once I had three daughters,' she told him, 'of whom the youngest was a vision of beauty, with her snow-white skin, cheeks like apple-blossom and hair as golden as sunlight. When she wept, pearls ran down her cheeks instead of salt tears.

'On her fifteenth birthday the king summoned our three daughters to the throne room.

'"The time has come for me to decide on your inheritance," he said. "I know you all love me, but she who loves me best will inherit the largest share." Turning to the eldest girl: "Tell me how much you love me," he said.

'"Oh, Father!" she cried, "I love you as much as the sweetest honey!"

'"And I," cried the second, "love you as much as a costly robe!"

'"Well, my dear child, how much do you love me?" asked the king, turning to the youngest.

'"I do not know," she said. "I have nothing to compare with my love for you."

'The king insisted on an answer and in the end the princess replied:

'"Even the best food is tasteless without salt. Therefore I love my father as much as salt!"

'At these words the king flew into a rage.

'"If salt is your answer, your inheritance shall be salty too!" he shouted.

'So he divided his kingdom between our elder daughters, but he ordered his men to take the youngest deep into the forest with a bag of salt on her back.

'We all pleaded for her,' sobbed the queen, 'but he was too angry to listen. How the poor child wept – the path was strewn with the pearls that flowed from her eyes! And when I saw the pearl in the box you gave me I knew it had something to do with our daughter. Please tell us how it came into your hands.'

The young nobleman told his story.

'The old woman was not wicked,' he added, 'but I believe she may be a good fairy. And I saw no sign of a beautiful princess.'

Nevertheless, the king and queen decided to return with him to the old woman's cottage, to seek news of their daughter.

Two days later, when the old crone was spinning in the dim evening light, the silence was broken by the honking of the geese returning from the meadow, with the goose-girl behind them. The old woman looked up without speaking and after a moment the hag sat down beside her and began to spin, her fingers flying like a young girl's.

Suddenly an owl appeared at the window, gazing in with its great yellow

eyes. It hooted three times, and at last the old woman spoke:

'Go, my child,' she said. 'It is time.'

The goose-girl got up and left the cottage. She walked down through the fields to the bottom of the valley and stopped at the foot of three great oaks. There, silvery under the full moon, flowed a crystal spring. The hag peeled off the hideous mask which covered her face, bowed her head over the water and washed herself. Then she washed the mask of skin and hung it up to dry by the light of the moon.

When she pulled a grey wig off her head a mass of golden hair tumbled onto her shoulders, her eyes sparkled like stars and her cheeks were as fresh as apple-blossom. Yet for all her beauty, the young girl was so sad that she began to weep, her tears running down her golden hair in a stream of pearls. She might have been there all night, if a sudden rustling in the leaves had not startled her. Nimble as a young doe, she snatched up the mask, and just as a cloud covered the moon, she pulled it over her head. When the moon reappeared, the girl had vanished.

It was the ugly hag who reached the cottage, shaking like a leaf. When she tried to tell the crone what had happened, the old woman smiled.

'I know all that!' she said, and picking up her broom she began to sweep the floor.

'Why are you working in the middle of the night, Mother?' asked the girl.

'It is nearly midnight,' said the crone. 'Do you know that three years have passed since you came to me, my child? Now it is time for you to go.'

'Oh, Mother dear,' cried the girl, 'do you want to get rid of me? Where shall I go? Do not send me away, I beg you!'

'I can't stay here much longer,' said the old woman, 'and I don't want to leave any untidiness behind. Don't worry – you will be well pleased with your wages!'

'Tell me what is to become of me!' the girl repeated.

'Not another word,' said the old woman. 'Go to your room, take off the mask and put on the silk dress you were wearing when you came here.'

Meanwhile, the young nobleman had been leading the king and queen towards the old woman's cottage, but they had become separated and now the young man was alone.

On the second day he recognised the countryside and walked on until evening, when he climbed a tree for the night. From the height of the tree he saw in the moonlight a figure coming down to the valley. It was the ugly goose-girl. He was just going to call out to her, when to his amazement he saw her pull off a mask of skin, wash herself in the spring and release a mass of golden hair from under a grey wig. Holding his breath, he stretched out along a branch, but his weight made the branch shake, and at the rustle of leaves the beautiful girl snatched up the mask and bounded away into the night.

The young man also ran across the fields, hoping to find her again, but the first people he saw were the king and queen, who had seen the light in the cottage window and were walking towards it.

The young man told them of
the miracle he had witnessed by
the spring and the three of them
hurried joyfully to the cottage.
The geese were asleep, nothing
moved. Looking through the
window, they saw an old woman
calmly spinning, in a room as
neat and bright as a new pin.

There was no sign of the princess.

When they knocked at the
door, the old woman opened it
with a smile.

'Come in,' she said. 'I have
been waiting for you.'

When they were inside, she
spoke again.

'You could have been spared
all this suffering if you had not
sent your daughter away for no
reason, three years ago. But she
has lacked for nothing, she has
looked after my geese, pure in
heart and safe from all evil. And
you have been punished enough
by your anguish.'

Turning away, she called:
'Come, my child, come!'

The door of the bedchamber opened and the princess appeared, wearing her silk dress. With her golden hair and shining eyes, she seemed like a being from heaven as she embraced her parents and all three wept for joy.

'Alas, my dear daughter,' said the king, 'I have given away my kingdom. There is nothing left for you.'

'She has all she needs!' said the old woman. 'I have gathered up the tears she has shed for you – they are the finest pearls, worth more than your kingdom. And she shall have my cottage as her wage.'

So saying, she vanished, the walls cracked open and the astonished girl saw that the little house had become a splendid palace.

There is more to the story, but I don't remember it very well. I think the beautiful princess must have married the young nobleman and lived with him in the palace for as long as it pleased God.

Perhaps those snow-white geese were really well-born maidens, and perhaps they became ladies-in-waiting to the young princess. I'm not sure, but it seems quite probable.

And perhaps the old woman really was a good fairy – the one who had bestowed on the infant princess the gift of weeping pearls.

Nowadays that wouldn't happen, but never mind – the poor can still get rich!

THE
KING
OF THE
GOLDEN
MOUNTAIN

There was once a rich merchant who had two children, a boy and a girl, whom he loved dearly. But when the children were still scarcely old enough to walk, his ships were lost in a storm and all that was left of his wealth was one field just outside the town.

The merchant took to walking in his field to clear his mind, but he could not throw off his worries and walked up and down, up and down, with an anxious frown on his face.

'Why so sad?' asked a gruff voice. The merchant looked down and saw a little man in black who seemed to have appeared out of the ground.

'Oh, if it would help, I would tell you,' said the merchant.

'Tell away,' said the little man. 'You never know.'

So the merchant told him that he had lost his fortune and had nothing left but this field to support himself and his family.

'Is that all?' said the little man in black. 'Just promise to bring me, in fifteen years' time, the first being to touch your leg when you go home and I will give you all the money you desire!'

The merchant agreed, feeling sure that his dog would come running out to meet him, but when he reached the house, his little boy was playing outside.

'Papa!' he cried and trotted unsteadily towards his father. Alas, he lost his balance and clutched at his father's leg as he fell. Only then did the poor man realise what he had done. He ran into the house and threw open his treasure chests. Empty! Perhaps it had all been a bad joke, after all?

One month later, all his money had gone and he prepared to sell his last pewter pots. But – oh, glory! – they were filled with gold. Soon the merchant was even richer than before, and he thanked God for His goodness.

Nevertheless, he did not forget his fatal agreement, and as the years passed his face grew grim with foreboding. His son asked what was causing him so much distress and at last the merchant confessed that he had made a bargain which would oblige him to give away his son in exchange for his fortune.

'That was certainly the devil,' said the boy. 'Do not worry, Papa, he has no power over me.' So saying, he went to see a priest, who gave him his blessing, and set off with his father on the appointed day. They drew a circle in the field, and father and son were standing inside it when the little man in black appeared.

'Have you brought me what you promised?' he growled.

But it was the boy who replied: 'You tricked my father. Release him from his contract!'

'Never!' cried the little man in black.

After long argument it was agreed that neither his father nor the devil should have the boy. Instead, he was to be set afloat, the merchant himself being the one to push the boat out to sea.

Father and son wept as they said goodbye, but the wretched merchant's sorrow turned to black despair as he saw the boat suddenly overturn. Sick at heart, he went home to mourn his dead son.

In fact, the boy was still safe and sound, sailing along inside the upturned boat. At last it was washed up at the foot of a mountain, on top of which stood a great castle. When the boy entered, he realised that this was an enchanted castle, standing quite empty in all its splendour, but for one hall, which was filled by a huge serpent.

'So, you have come at last, my deliverer!' hissed the serpent sweetly. 'Fifteen years ago a wicked wizard turned me into a snake, and you alone can break the spell that keeps me prisoner!'

'How am I to do that?' asked the boy.

'Tonight twelve men laden with chains will come and ask what you are doing here. Do not answer them! They will beat you and stick their daggers into you, but you must remain silent. They will depart at midnight, but tomorrow twelve more will come, and on the third night, twenty-four. This time, they will cut off your head.

'But at midnight they will lose their power for ever, and if you have endured it all without uttering a single word, I shall be free. Once in my human form, I will sprinkle you with my elixir of life and you will be safe and sound again!'

'I will withstand all these trials to set you free,' said the young man.

Everything happened as the serpent had foretold. The wicked little men did their worst, but the young man did not speak or cry out, and at midnight on

the third night the spell was broken and the snake turned back into a beautiful princess. With her magic elixir she brought the young man back to life and they fell in love and married. On their wedding day the young man became King of the Golden Mountain. When the queen gave birth to a son a year later, their happiness was complete.

Eight years passed and the king's longing to see his father grew so great that he decided to find the way to his former home and bring his parents back to live with them. But the queen was troubled.

'I fear that this will put an end to our happiness,' she told her husband. 'But since you insist, here is a magic ring. Turn it, and you can travel, or make others travel, wherever you wish. But you must never use it to bring me to your father!'

By this means the king was able to travel immediately to the gates of the town where his parents lived, but to his surprise the guards would not admit him. The splendour and strangeness of his robes had aroused their suspicion, so he went into the countryside and changed clothes with a shepherd, after which he was allowed to enter the town.

His difficulties were not over, however, for the merchant and his wife refused to recognize him. The king was bewildered.

'Isn't there some birthmark by which you could recognize me?' he asked.

'Ah yes,' sighed his mother. 'Our little boy had a raspberry-shaped mark under his right arm.'

The shepherd-king pulled up his sleeves and showed them the mark; he was indeed their son. But he was now also a king, and his parents would not believe that, either.

His indignation making him forget his promise, the king turned his ring and ordered the queen and prince to be brought to him.

They appeared at once, but the queen was in tears. 'You have broken your word to me,' she cried. 'Our happiness is at an end.'

'Truly, I meant no harm,' said the king. 'I was confused. Forgive me!'

He comforted his wife with many tender words, but at the bottom of her heart she was still angry.

He took the queen and prince to the field where the whole story had begun, and showed them where his boat had left the shore. Then, tired out, he lay down with his head in his wife's lap and fell asleep.

Very gently, the queen drew the magic ring off his finger, put her shoe under his head for a pillow and wished herself and the little prince back in their palace.

When the king woke up he realized at once what had happened.

'I cannot go to my parents now,' he said. 'This is really too much for them to believe! I shall have to return to my kingdom on foot.'

After a long walk the king came upon three giants who were quarrelling over their inheritance.

'Ha!' cried one, 'here is one of the little people. They are said to be quick-witted – let us ask him to help us.'

Their father had left them a sword, a cloak and a pair of boots. The owner of the sword had only to say: 'Heads off, all but mine!' and all his enemies' heads would roll on the ground. The owner of the cloak had only to throw it over his shoulders and he would be invisible. And the boots would carry their owner wherever he wished.

'Give me the things,' said the king. 'They must first be tested.' The giants gave him the cloak, he threw it over his shoulders, and vanished.

'The cloak works well,' he said, removing it. 'Now for the sword.'

'No, no,' said the giants, 'for if you said "Heads off!" we would all be dead.'

The king promised not to use the magic words and tested the sword on a tree trunk, which snapped like a straw.

'Let's have a look at the boots,' he said – but he had not returned the cloak or the sword.

'No,' said the giants, 'for if you put them on and said, "Set me down on that hill!" we would be left empty-handed.'

'I shan't say that!' said the king, and it was quite true, for as soon as he had slipped into the huge boots, he said: 'Set me down on the Golden Mountain!' Now king and cloak and sword and boots had vanished. He had solved the problem of the giants' inheritance, to be sure.

Once in his kingdom, the king was surprised to hear sounds of singing and dancing. 'The queen is getting married again!' the people cried.

'Faithless woman!' cried the king. 'First she deserts me, then she deceives me!'

Throwing the cloak over his shoulders, he entered the palace unseen and found the queen seated on the throne, her courtiers feasting about her. Every time a footman served her with food or wine, the invisible King of the Golden Mountain took them away from her.

The queen was frightened, and then ashamed. Perhaps God was punishing her for her treachery? She ran to her room, followed by the king.

'Is the devil tormenting me?' she cried. 'Oh, what has become of my deliverer?'

'Here is your deliverer!' cried the king, throwing off his cloak of invisibility. 'What have I done to deserve such treatment?'

Returning to the throneroom, he shouted:

'There will be no wedding. The true king has returned!'

The kings, princes and noblemen invited to the feast burst out laughing, and some drew their swords, but the king's sword was a match for them.

'Heads off, all but mine!' he shouted, and at once all their heads were rolling on the ground. After so many adventures, he was King of the Golden Mountain again. Forgiven and forgiving, he reigned with his queen until the time came for their son to rule the kingdom in his turn.